WARNING

This book contains sexually explicit scenes and adult language. It may be considered offensive to some readers. This book is for sale to adults ONLY.

* * * * * * * * * * * * * * * *

Please store your files wisely where they cannot be accessed by underage readers.

ISBN-13: 978-1988083865
ISBN-10: 1988083869

Other Books by Darla Dunbar:

<u>The Romeo Alpha BBW Paranormal Shifter Romance Series</u> (This series precedes the "<u>Romeo Alpha Blood Lines Romance Series</u>")

Amanda Walker thinks that she has a normal and boring life. That is until after her 24th birthday. Everything changes when she meets the man who says he was supposed to be her husband. Denying everything the man says, she fights him every step of the way. But after he kidnaps her, Amanda discovers that there are some things about her family that her parents kept a secret all these years. Among the history of the family she learns secrets she thought only happened in story books. Can Amanda tell the difference between truth and lies or is she this mysterious woman that holds the key to a legacy?

<u>The Alpha Feud BBW Paranormal Shifter Romance Series</u>

Eliza's life consisted of reporting on boring, crowd-pleasing events, like their country livestock fair. With the arrival of two handsome brothers, the lives of Eliza and her best friend, Melissa, are shaken to the core. For Eliza, the arrival of this new man becomes a test of her relationship with her current boyfriend, who she's been happily living with for over six years. Does Hayden, a complete stranger, really wield the power to make Eliza reconsider her relationship with Andrew?

<u>The Alpha Packed BBW Paranormal Shifter Romance Series</u>

Darlene has led a quiet life since suffering through a terrible break-up. She wants nothing more than to spend her time in front of the TV, away from any sort of trouble. But all that goes down the drain when handsome, rugged and rough Idris comes into her life. He is a werewolf on the lookout for his missing pack leader. Darlene quickly finds herself pulled towards this mysterious man and at the same time finds herself falling deeper and deeper into the world of the supernatural.

<u>The Daemon Paranormal Romance Chronicles</u>

The daemon infighting can only be stopped when a strong leader emerges to calm the different factions. Juno appears to be at the heart of the conflict. Things become complicated when Phoebe and Supay try to negotiate with the siren, Juno. The love triangle among Phoebe, Supay and Apollo become tense when Juno's meddling threatens to destroy any romance that develops.

<u>The Mind Talker Paranormal Romance Series</u>

Ananda finds herself on the run and she's not alone. With help from Jared, a stranger that she just met, the two evade capture by an organization that is intent on hunting her kind. Ananda and Jared are able to read minds. When an unfortunate incident happened involving a disturbed individual that resulted in the death of his schoolmates, the secret organization decided to take action.

This book is Part One of the "Romeo Alpha Blood Lines Romance Series" and follows twenty-four years after "The Romeo Alpha BBW Paranormal Shifter Romance Series"

1 - Blood Lines

Twenty-four years have passed in relative peace for Amanda and Romeo. They've raised five children into adulthood and are thoroughly enjoying their lives as the Alpha King and Queen of the werewolves. At twenty-four, Sarina is just stepping into her powers and will be ripe for mating when her birthday comes in two weeks. What no one knows is the danger that lurks just outside their tight knit community. Romeo has made peace with the other clans and has enjoyed that peace, but it will all come crashing down around him when his oldest daughter comes of age to take a mate.

2 - Alpha Infiltration

Brody is an attentive and loving mate and Sarina finds herself engulfed by the love of her family. When things start to change with the twins though, Sarina finds herself torn in two. She loves Brody in a way she's never loved another man, human or wolf. When he shows signs of the dark void, however, she can't decide whether to run from him or to him. She's frightened for both of her sons and struggles with her own mortality.

3 - Alpha Bait

Lilith is on the loose, plotting and planning with Fenris to take down the Delta pack and its alpha, Romeo. Sarina and Brody have their work cut out for them in order to stop the hostile takeover. With their wedding on the horizon, both feel compelled to spend time with their family even as danger lurks around every corner. When the twin babies, Jedidiah and Brody Jr., go missing, all hands are on deck to search for the leaders of the next generation of the Delta pack. And as Sarina and Brody dig deeper into Lilith's past, especially where Romeo is concerned, they find a mind twisted by deception and an overly unhealthy obsession with power.

4 - Alpha Strategy

With Lilith's soul separated from her body, Romeo and Amanda are bent on seeing her body destroyed so that she never comes back again. What they've forgotten in the meantime is that Lilith wasn't alone in her desire over control of the Delta pack and Romeo. Sarina and Brody are finally enjoying a quiet life, not that they expect it to last long. Their wedding, a source of great stress, is just weeks away. With all that's going on though, Sarina wonders if she'll ever be able to legally wed her mate.

5 - Alpha Revelation

Lilith has haunted the Traverse family since the beginning but her obsession with the reigning alpha and his immediate family is more than Romeo's eldest daughter can stand. In a twisted allegiance with her first mate, Fenris, Lilith has caused unbearable pain to the Delta pack's community and now she has gone as far as to make a deal with the Devil. She has comfortably inhabited Sarina's body, playing wife to Brody and

mother to the couple's twin boys. Digging her way up
from Hell wasn't easy, but Sarina harnesses powers that
rival even those of her mother.

Alpha Romeo Blood Lines Romance Series

Blood Lines

Book One

By Darla Dunbar

Copyright Revelry Publishing 2016

Table of Contents

Chapter One

ROMEO AND his lovely wife, Amanda, walked the land just outside of their home. Over the last quarter century, they'd purchased hundreds of acres, building on the property borders that Jeremiah, Romeo's father, had purchased before they were born.

"It's lovely this time of day, before the sun wakes."

"It's lovely any morning I get to walk with you," Romeo said, pressing a kiss to Amanda's temple. Neither of them had aged poorly. Romeo was still tall, well-muscled, and ruggedly handsome. His hair, a light brown, was just starting to gray at the temples, making Amanda only more attracted to her sexy husband. He still wore it long, pulling it back into a ponytail because he knew she loved it that way. His blue eyes, still clear and beautiful, smiled at her. "Does that get me brownie points?"

"Only because you're so damned sexy," Amanda grinned. She wore her dark hair pulled into a circle braid and pinned down, knowing full well her husband liked to nuzzle her neck. She liked to let him. "Sarina will become a breeder in two weeks." Amanda didn't need to look at her husband to know his whole body went tense with protectiveness for his oldest daughter.

"I don't want to think about it. I remember what I was like with you. She won't be taking an alpha as a mate and I don't want to talk about it."

"Like it or not, it is something we should discuss. I don't want her brothers thinking that they can keep her under lock and key. We've raised her to be a confident and independent woman."

"And?" Romeo said, hating the logic in his wife's words.

"And, we have to have faith that we raised her right. She's not without her own set of defenses you know," Amanda grinned.

"Yes," Romeo sighed. "Jason, Wade and Joshua."

"More like her powers of witchcraft and her wolf."

"They aren't enough," Romeo growled.

"They'll have to be," Amanda said wisely. "I didn't even know I had powers until my twenty-fourth year. At least she's going into this knowing how it will be for her."

"She's never changed before. With her first full moon coming up, I don't like the idea that all the males in our community will sniff her out."

"We can't keep them away forever, Love. We can, however, continue to give her the tools she needs to choose wisely."

"I didn't let you choose," Romeo said, his blue eyes pensive.

"I don't believe I would have chosen differently, even if I'd been offered someone else as my mate. I was made for you, remember?"

"I'd remember easier if you'd let me have you." Amanda giggled and ran as Romeo got that needy look in his eyes. She loved that look, the one that said simply, *I want you, now.* She played cat and mouse with him for a time before she let him catch her and remind her of what it'd been like when she was twenty-four.

Sarina grinned after besting her twin, Jason, in racquetball. They'd begged and begged their parents for a racquetball court and finally for their eighteenth birthdays, they'd been given their present. The walls were well worn where they'd also played wally ball during inclement weather, when neither the wolves in them, nor their human selves wanted to go outside.

"You just can't win baby brother," Sarina laughed.

"My ass," Jason pouted. *Princess* Sarina never missed an opportunity to rub in the fact that she was older by all of five minutes. "I can best you any time I wish."

"Ha, you can't tell me you let me win every time. Remember brother, we shared the same womb. I know you better than you know yourself."

"Not likely," Jason scoffed. "You have no idea what it's like for me to be with a woman."

Despite the blush that crept along her cheeks, Sarina laughed. "No, but it won't be long now before I find out what it's like to be with a man."

The growl came fast and furious as Jason bared his teeth at the mention of Sarina mating. She'd expected as much and just rolled her eyes. "Ease off J, I haven't taken a man to my bed, yet."

This time when he growled, Sarina grinned when Romeo set a firm hand on his shoulder. "Don't antagonize your brother Sarina. You know he'd rip out the throat of any man who touched you, especially against your will."

"Yes I do, but it's so much fun, Dad."

"Maybe so," Romeo grinned, knowing his two oldest children well. He never told them they were more alike than they were different. Both were fiercely loyal to the other, as well as their family. Both valued the other's opinions, and both would give their lives in protection of their womb-mate, or any member of their family. "But your mother and I appreciate the peace that has finally settled over our house."

Just then, they heard screaming coming from the kitchen. "You were saying?" Amanda giggled. Everyone else followed her into the large kitchen that Romeo had upgraded upon Amanda taking over her

Aunt Mabel's mansion. Mabel Walker had been an intensely loyal woman. So loyal in fact that she'd had a hysterectomy to ensure that no wolf would have the say over her breeding rights. She'd let the Walker and Traverse lines and legacies pass on to Amanda, even to the extent of making Amanda believe that she had no other family to care for her after her parents had been killed.

"You son-of-a—"

"I'll thank you not to finish that sentence as I'm the woman who birthed you both," Amanda said, her voice firm.

"Sorry, Mama. But you didn't see what Joshua did!" Shawna whined. At nineteen she was just becoming the woman they'd raised her to be. Still five years off from her own breeding season start, she had much to learn.

"I don't need to see what he did to know that somehow it hurt your feelings."

"She's as sensitive as a new pup," Joshua smirked before getting a thump on the head from his father. "Ow!"

"Tell your sister you're sorry," Romeo warned. "She shared the womb with you, Joshua. Try to remember that when you start bickering and wanting to tease her."

"But she—" Joshua defended himself.

"Whatever you two did to each other doesn't matter now. I can, however, promise that it will matter tonight at supper if you two don't straighten it out."

The twins groaned through their apologies and then went their separate ways. "They're just like you, you know," Amanda chuckled.

"Oh, no. Those two are absolutely yours."

"That they are. I wouldn't have it any other way." Amanda allowed Romeo to pull her into his arms, kissing her soundly. Had it really been nearly twenty-four years since she'd brought their two oldest children into the world? Regardless, the day had been one for their personal history books and he was still just as handsome as she remembered.

Brody Duscene paced back and forth in his home. He could feel the full moon rising, the urge to change gnawing at him ferociously. Panting as it rose high in the sky, he felt the change begin. The searing pain of it ran through his blood and into his bones as they began to lengthen and shift. He bent down to his knees as his hands and feet turned to five-toed paws and his clothes tore away as long, gray fur grew thick over his body.

It always occurred to him after the change that he'd save himself some considerable money if he'd learn to strip before the change, but regardless of the countless times it'd happened since his eighteenth birthday, he had yet to take to the change without his clothes on. The last part to change and always the most painful was his face. His nose lengthened and flattened as his cheek bones and jaw became a muzzle. His tongue grew longer and thinner and his eyes became a keen and sensitive part of his five senses. Within mere minutes he'd become a werewolf and would hunt his prey like a predator, with stealth and a vicious appetite.

Brody waited near a clump of trees as a young couple necked in a car near a stretch of abandoned road. His eyes were barely slits as he watched them. Their soft whispers were easy for his big ears to hear and made the man inside the wolf horny as hell. He always felt guilty when hunting humans, but it was a necessity in order to be a member of Reggie's pack. There were other packs that strictly prohibited the hunting of humans, but switching packs wasn't as easy as changing shirts.

Knowing full well the two love birds in his sights were focused elsewhere, Brody approached the car slowly, sniffing their scents and imprinting them in his memory. If one tried to run, he'd find them. Grabbing the door handle, Brody ripped the door away. He yanked the boy out of the car as the girl screamed. Turning his head back to her, Brody bared his teeth in a snarl that had the girl stumbling away from the car as she attempted to run. Brody let her go, knowing he'd find her when he was done with the boy.

Unlike some in his pack, Brody wasn't one to play with his food. Nor was he the type to hunt with other wolves. He preferred to hunt solo. Whatever he caught was his own. He knew the boundaries of his pack; had been taught them from a pup. But the difference between Brody and the other young wolves in his pack was that Brody *didn't care* about boundaries. Who'd know if he stepped over his section of the world?

Every full moon from the spring equinox, Brody had been exploring regions beyond where his pack lived and hunted. He didn't like hunting in his pack's territory where he'd grown familiar with the local human population. In order to hunt humans he wouldn't get a chance to know, he had to escape the confines Reggie had set for them. Brody was smart enough to know that he wasn't near ready to challenge Reggie for the alpha position of their pack, but soon, very soon, he'd be more than ready.

"Please doggie," the boy in his grip pleaded. The hardest part of the hunt was when his prey begged. Without hesitating much longer, he sank his teeth into the soft flesh of the boy's neck. Blood, rich and full of flavor, rushed past his throat and soaked into his muzzle as he feasted. Brody didn't toy with the humans he preyed upon. Being partly human himself, it always felt like a kick to the teeth to watch another wolf do it, so Brody hunted, ate, and left his carcasses in peace when he was done. He finished the boy with relative ease, licking his lips clean. Returning to the car he picked up the girl's scent and howled at the full moon as he sniffed her out.

Twenty minutes later he found her hovering in the lower branches of an oak tree. He gave her props for being smart enough to climb a tree so he left her there and lay down to sleep. When he woke the next morning naked and sleepy, Brody looked up to see the woman watching him. Smiling, he waved to her before he took off at a sprint. If Reggie caught him outside their boundaries there'd be hell to pay and Brody just wasn't in the mood today.

"Happy Birthday!"

Sarina heard from everyone as she blew out her birthday candles. Across from her Jason did the same thing. Growing up, they'd always kept the same tradition. Always facing each other and blowing out their candles together as everyone yelled their birthday wishes.

"Can you believe it?" she said to Jason later when their extended family and friends had finally gone home. "We're twenty-four."

"It's just another year, Sis," Jason said, blowing it off and irritating her.

"The hell it is. It's my first breeding year buddy. Just because you don't give a shit, doesn't mean I shouldn't."

"Look, just because you're in an all fire hurry to blow your virginal attributes, doesn't mean that I have to run around as if I've never been laid before."

Sarina snarled at him and stalked off. Finding her mother alone, she sat down on her parent's bed.

"What was it like for you, Mama, when you turned twenty-four?"

"Different from what you're experiencing, I can tell you that," Amanda said as she hung Romeo's dress shirts in the closet. "For starters, when I turned twenty-four I had no idea that I was a werewolf nor a witch. I came to claim my Aunt Mabel's estate and was accosted by your father, who back then was not a people person. He demanded that I marry him and was all too forthcoming with details I didn't want to hear."

"Dad really did that?"

Amanda laughed. "That and more, sweetheart."

"You were a virgin?"

"Yes," Amanda replied. Sarina could tell by the way her mother was eyeing her that she should explain herself.

"I'm nervous," she continued, rushing through the details as if she couldn't breathe. "I don't even have a wolf or man who's interested in me, but I know they will be once they learn I'm in season and especially an alpha's daughter."

"The right man won't care whether you're an alpha's daughter or not. He'll want you for certain, but he'll also care about the woman inside the wolf."

"Did Dad care?"

"In his own way," Amanda smiled. "Like you, we were both young and had less control than we'd probably have liked."

"Is it normal to be scared?"

"Yes," Amanda chuckled. Sarina let her mother pull her into her arms. "Your first time will be something to remember, surely. Just try to remember as well that you don't have to rush. The full moon is nearly a month away and you won't go into season until then. There's still time, especially as werewolves tend to come together in whirlwind circumstances."

"Uncle Elijah and Aunt Penelope didn't," Sarina countered. She knew she was being difficult, but without any prospects and on the day of her twenty-fourth birthday she was feeling edgy.

"Your aunt and uncle certainly did come together in a whirlwind," Amanda explained. "It just so happens that they only thought they couldn't be together. When I became the leading Radiant, I changed the law so that Radiants could marry the loves of their hearts. I didn't want anyone, especially my fellow Radiants, to suffer their hearts for the duties of their souls."

"I hope I'm half the leader you are if it's ever my turn."

"As the oldest, the leadership of the witches would pass to you. However, you could choose to pass it on to Jason if you felt he'd do a better job."

"Not if he doesn't get his head out of his ass," Sarina scoffed.

"And just think. I'd hoped by now you two would have stopped the petty bickering. Aren't there bigger things to worry about?"

"According to him, I'm in an all fired hurry to lose my virginity. Doesn't he know what it's like? Certainly he had a first time too."

"Men rarely see those things the same way as women, darling."

"Still, he could be a little understanding."

"Oh just wait until a man starts sniffing around you. You'll find out how fast your brothers will defend you, even when you wish they wouldn't. Not just Jason either. Wade and Joshua will protect you with the fierceness of our kind. Even Shawna would come to your defense if she was needed."

"Great," Sarina moped. "First I'm a slut, because I want to talk about it. Now I'll have to beat my siblings off the poor man with a stick."

"Who knows, maybe they'll be in the mood to play fetch."

"You always know what to say to make me feel better." Sarina laughed and thanked her mother for the talk.

"It is a skill I learned over time. You will too, darling."

Chapter Two

Brody woke that afternoon and dressed in fresh clothes. He'd barely made it back for check-in time to beat Reggie. Thankfully he had as it would have been painful to have missed the morning after curfew. Reggie was a bastard when it came to controlling their pack. He was so paranoid about running into other packs that he forbade anyone from wandering farther than their borders. Now Brody certainly wasn't going to volunteer the information to the old man, but he did like to play with him once in a while.

"Get up pup," the old man called.

"I'm up, Reggie," Brody countered.

"Good," he returned. "I have a job for you."

"Name it."

"Did you eat well last night?"

"My wolf is comfortable and quiet, for now."

"Excellent. It will aid you in today's assignment as I need my sharpest wolf on the job."

"What is it I'm going to be doing?"

"I need you to go into town and pick up a truckload of supplies. Don't talk to anyone except the clerk at the hardware store. The less interaction you have, the less likely anyone is to suspect you're anything other than a lad picking up supplies."

Brody left an hour later, making it to town in record time. He didn't often drive Reggie's coupe, but when he did it was fast, with the pedal to the floor. He parked easily in front of Tate's Hardware. Taking the invoice in, he took possession of the freight Reggie had ordered. He hooked the trailer up to the coupe and wondered why in the hell the old man had put a towing hitch on the car instead of buying a truck for this sort of need. Figuring he'd earned it, Brody strolled down the sidewalk to the bar. He ordered a beer and sat outside to enjoy the view of the people who walked by. He smiled, thinking maybe he'd come closer to town on the next full moon. Some of the people smelled divine.

Just as he was finishing his beer, however, Brody picked up a smell that was beyond divine. Exotic and overtly female… whoever she was, she had Brody's system in overdrive within seconds. Tossing his beer bottle aside, he followed the scent to a small, upscale boutique and waited. He knew she was inside, probably flipping through frilly dresses. Her smell saturated his senses until Brody caught the strong hint of wolf. Could it be a female werewolf inside? He could smell her pheromones as if they'd been intimate. Already revved, Brody clamped down his arousal. The last thing he needed to do was chase her home and have her running through town screaming about a stalker. Reggie would certainly punish him for that. However, given the woman's overdriven body, she just might be worth it in the long run.

Brody waited so long that the wolf inside the man began to slumber, losing the scent of the woman. Still, he held tight to the traces of it and an hour later she finally emerged from the shop, a large bag in her hand. Brody practically licked his lips just looking at her. Tall and lean with legs up to her ears, the woman in front of him oozed sex from every pore on her body. Her hair was long and blonde with just enough wave to make his hands ache to touch it. He thought fleetingly about whistling at her, but decided a catcall would do disservice to his ability to watch her. And watch her he did, almost to the point of forgetting the shipment he was meant to bring back to Reggie.

"Excuse me," he found himself saying.

She turned around and practically had Brody tripping over his own tongue. "Yes?"

"I couldn't help but notice you came out of that boutique back there. Is that a store that sells just clothes and accessories for women, or do they sell men's clothing as well?"

Sarina had heard some terrible pick-up lines in her day, but this one might just take the cake. "It's a female-oriented store I guess you'd say, but I suppose there might be something there for men as well."

"Great, thanks."

Sarina watched the gorgeous man turn away and bit her lip, debating whether to engage him again.

"I'm Sarina." This time when he turned around, Sarina caught the gleam in his pretty blue eyes and grinned. Sexy didn't begin to touch this male specimen and Sarina found her now ripe system revved and slipping into drive.

"It's very nice to meet you Sarina," he smiled. "I'm Brody Duscene."

"It's nice to meet you as well, Brody Duscene," Sarina smiled. "Do you live around these parts?"

"I live close enough, although it's a ways off, even by car."

"Oh," she said, disappointed.

"Listen, I have a delivery to make, but would you like to meet me back here tonight for dinner?"

"I'd like that very much." Sarina smiled. She let Brody kiss her hand and swore she felt him breathe her in as he did so. If she wasn't mistaken and her senses told her she wasn't, Brody Duscene was a werewolf, and one who she knew, didn't belong to her father's pack.

As long as she could remember, she'd been all but paraded in front of the boys in her father's pack as a sort of prize. He didn't go as far as to promise her to any one of them in particular, but they all understood that someday she'd be of age for breeding. She was in effect, like a prime piece of real estate that every male in her pack wanted to stake their claim on. The only problem was that Sarina knew all the men in her father's pack and none of them came close to affecting her the way that Brody Duscene did. Smiling, she knew her mother had been right. She'd known from the moment she'd seen him, sensed him, that this was the man she'd been waiting for. Now it was up to her, as an alpha's daughter, to help him come to the same conclusion. She was the first daughter of the Western Pack. Brody Duscene was as good as sunk, even if he didn't know it yet.

"Where are you going?" Jason asked, a note of irritation in his voice when he saw her dressed up.

"I have a date."

"With who?" Jason asked, a low growl emanating from his throat. "I know all our males and none has shown an interest in you, no offense."

"This wolf isn't from our pack. He was in town today when I was shopping. He asked me out to dinner and I agreed."

"Dad won't like this, Sarina."

"I'm past the point of caring what dad does and doesn't like. I'm twenty-four and if I'm going to ensure the advancement of our species to the next generation, it's time I looked out for myself."

"Let me at least tag along at a distance."

"Do you think I can't fend for myself? Dad taught us both how to use our skills to protect ourselves. Even being naïve about sex doesn't make me defenseless." Sarina bared her canine teeth for emphasis.

"You said this guy was a wolf as well. Does he know you know that?"

"I didn't announce it," Sarina said, her dark eyes focused, serious. "Contrary to popular belief I do know how to keep some things to myself."

"Good. If he thinks you see him as just another human, you'll have the advantage. But I can guarantee Dad will send one of us along as a chaperone. Breeding or not, Dad isn't going to let just anyone slip into our pack and have you."

Sarina blushed. It was one thing to discuss sex in the abstract. It was another all together to have her brother discuss it. "Fine, but keep your distance and don't you dare embarrass me. I have a right to my own life, no matter what you or Dad think."

Brody made sure Reggie was well preoccupied with other matters, namely Alyssa, before he left the cave. He worked his way around, sure to leave his scent in several different spots, in case he missed curfew, so they wouldn't be able to track him at first. He made it to town just after seven, the time he'd agreed to meet Sarina at Rick's Oyster Bar.

"You made it!" she beamed, her pretty, dark eyes smiling at him. Brody smiled back and waved. Brody met her at the table and kissed her cheek in greeting.

"You look amazing," he said, appreciating just how good she looked. She paired a set of skinny jeans with a hot pink see-through shirt. She'd put a white tank underneath that showed off plenty of curve. Brody could already feel his system turning on. He couldn't wait to see her wolf come out. If she was smoking hot as a human, he could only imagine what her wolf looked like. Sleek and stylish, even for a dog of legend, for there wasn't a wolf within the country, let alone the Delta that didn't know of Sarina's father and grandfather. Jeremiah and his son Romeo's fame stretched well into the hidden countryside and even beyond as the peace he'd brought settled nicely over the Delta region.

"Thanks," Sarina smiled. "Just to be clear, I'm one for being extremely upfront and in-your-face-plain-speaking. I like to get things out in the open."

"Alright," Brody grinned. "Is there something in particular you wanted to get out in the open, or were you just warning me?"

"Actually," she said, leaning closer in, conspiratorially. "I'd really, really like to know what you look like when you shift."

Brody didn't let his surprise show. If he could smell her a mile away, it stood to reason that she had also deduced his nature as well. Still, her answer intrigued him. Unlike the females in his pack, Sarina was exceptional. A put-it-all-out-there sort of woman. That was something Brody liked very much. "Well we certainly can't do that here," he smiled. "But there are other places that lend themselves to getting our wolf on. I was thinking as I sat down that your wolf must be sleek and stylish."

"I certainly hope she's sleek and stylish," Sarina smiled. "Maybe I'll be lucky enough to have a coat like my hair, blondish with streaks of the dark hair I get from my mother. I just hope the change isn't unbearable."

"And your mother is?"

"Oh, I forgot that you aren't from our pack. Her name is Amanda Walker Traverse. She is the ruling queen and wife to my dad, Romeo."

"Your dad is Romeo?" Brody asked, pretending not to know already.

"Yes," Sarina smiled. "But don't worry. He realizes that at twenty-four I've reached my first breeding season and will undoubtedly attract a number of would-be suitors."

"Is that what this is?" Brody said, wondering at the sudden irritation that slammed through his system. "Is this a sort of try-out? To see if I fit the bill as a future son-in-law?"

"No," Sarina said, her dark chocolate eyes blazing. "I like you. I thought we could get to know each other a little better. Obviously I was mistaken."

She stood up quickly, faster and more elegant than he'd given her credit for. "Sarina," he called as she stalked away, every bit the lustrous predator. Slipping a fifty onto the table, Brody followed her, running to catch her once she was outside the restaurant.

"Sarina!" Brody caught up with her with some trying on his part and felt the hard sting of her palm across his face when he grabbed her arm. "Jesus!"

"How dare you think that I agreed to this date as a *try-out*."

"What the hell was I supposed to think? You go off halfcocked, spouting about your parentage. Your dad is the alpha of nearly the entire valley and I'm not just supposed to believe that he won't kill me for even looking twice at you?"

"You're supposed to know I'm a grown woman, capable of making my own decisions. Capable of choosing for myself who interests me and who doesn't. I may be his eldest daughter and this may be my first season, but that doesn't mean that I haven't spent years deciding what it is I want and need in a mate. I'm sorry I obviously wasted your time. I'll be going now."

"The hell you will," Brody said. Grabbing her hand, Brody pulled her to him, his lips crushing hers in a heated kiss. His attraction to her punched him so fast in the gut that it stole his breath away. He pulled back and looked into Sarina's equally shocked eyes. He kissed her again, this time going slow and savoring the way she trembled against him. She opened to him easily, eagerly seeking the tongue he slid past her lips.

He couldn't remember the last time he'd kissed a woman like Sarina, if ever. She didn't hold back, or use her body as a toy to tease him. She simply gave and took in equal measure. Brody let his hands travel up her back, waking the nerves along her spine. Her hair felt like silk when his fingers sank into the long locks that cascaded down her back and the soft growl in her throat only heightened Brody's awareness of her.

Sarina had been waiting for this for what seemed like forever, to feel this alive at a man's touch. She wasn't a prude, or at least she didn't think she was. Nor was she one to take her love life for granted, such as it is. She'd always been careful with who she let get closer. Somehow though, this frustratingly wonderful man had slipped past her defenses. He overwhelmed her common sense with quick wit and even quicker moves. The way his lips roamed over hers as if she were a feast to be savored made her head spin.

"Wait," she breathed. "Brody, wait."

"Is there something wrong?" he asked, his blue eyes dark and dangerously needy.

"It's just… I don't want to move too fast in this relationship."

"Not even if it's the relationship you've been waiting for?" Sarina didn't want to visit how he knew her feelings, nor was she about to ask. "Your eyes give you away darling."

"No I just," Sarina sighed. "Shit. Suddenly I feel all the weight of our kind, as if I'm the single thread holding it all together."

"Maybe you are," Brody said with a grin on his face. "Does it seem so wrong to hold us all together, with me?"

"It's not that," Sarina tried to explain. "You know about breeders, right? About their first year in season?"

"If you're asking if I know the details of a breeder's rightful passage once their twenty-fourth birthday comes around, then yes, I know."

"Okay so, as you can imagine my parents, particularly my dad and my three brothers, have all kept a very strict and watchful eye on me. I've never dated, never gone out with anyone of the opposite sex, until today. I'm surprised that one of them hasn't shown up, chasing me down, yet."

"Do you expect them to?"

"Yes, actually," Sarina chuckled. "They're a bit neurotic when it comes to me and my chastity."

"And you think they'd be pissed if they saw us together?"

"Pissed doesn't even cover it."

"Do you want to be with me?" asked Brody, his eyebrows raised.

Sarina thought about his question and realized that therein lay the crux of the problem. Here stood a man that everything in her wanted. She could rationalize all day long about the pros and cons of taking their acquaintance further, but would it really change what she wanted?

"Yes," she nearly whispered. She let Brody take her hands in his as the inquiring look on his face softened.

"Alright then," he said, smiling. God he was sexy. She could just imagine what his wolf looked like. Dark and dangerous, like him. Were his eyes also blue when he wasn't hunting? "How about we get to know each other. Can you meet me here tomorrow?"

"Yeah," Sarina said as a smile lit up her face.

"Good," he grinned. "And Sarina?"

"Yeah?"

"Lose whoever it is that's tailing us."

Instantly Sarina remembered Jason. "Alright."

"What the hell was all of that?" Jason said, interrogating his sister as soon as they were on their own land again.

"Leave off, Jason."

"The hell I will," he said, stopping her retreat with a hand on her arm.

"Let go of me," Sarina growled, her fangs glinting in the moonlight.

"Oh put your teeth away, no one's about to lynch you. We've all had our days of fun."

"That's it, isn't it? You, Wade, even Joshua get to trample around here taking any number of females to your bed. You play around as if the world is at your feet just waiting for you to dictate what you want. Then I find a guy who's interested in more than just getting in my pants, and its doomsday."

"It's not like that, Sarina. But I'm your twin. Of course it's going to be odd when a guy shows more than a passing interest."

"Fine, but you have to lay off. I'm a grown woman now, whether anyone in this house wants to acknowledge that fact or not."

"No one's arguing differently."

"Good. Then from now on you let me be my own person. Don't follow me again Jason."

"Can't do it, Sis. You know Dad would literally have my hide if I let anything happen to you. Especially if I knew about the situation before hand."

"Then I won't tell you." Sarina pushed his arm back and kept going toward their house.

"Not so fast. Tell me what?"

"Nothing," she said smugly.

"Tell me or I'll let Dad know that a guy, one who doesn't belong to our pack, is sniffing around you."

"You wouldn't."

"I don't want to, but if it comes down to what I perceive as your safety, then, yes I would."

"Bastard," Sarina sighed. "Fine. Brody asked me to meet him tomorrow. No, I won't tell you the time or place."

"Fine," Jason said. "But you know I'm going to tail you. I have to, Sarina, for your safety and my own."

"Oh please," she argued. "You're Dad's golden boy. We all know you'll take over as alpha when his time is done."

"That being the case or not, if I let something happen to you, it'll be a long, long time before Dad steps down."

Sarina rolled her eyes. "Excuses, excuses."

The next morning, Sarina showered after a hard workout. She wore a cute sundress with hot pink strappy sandals and hooped earrings to match. She put her hair up in an easy ponytail and sprayed on perfume before she headed downstairs. "You look nice today," Romeo said. Sarina smiled.

"Thanks Daddy," she cooed. "You don't look half bad yourself."

"He looks way better than half bad," Amanda smiled, leaning over to kiss her husband.

"So what do you have planned for the day?"

"Just hanging out with some friends."

"Do I know these friends?"

"Dad, really? I'm twenty-four. Is it realistic to think you'll know everyone I hang out with?"

"No, but it's realistic to think you'll take one of your brothers with you."

"Come on, Dad!" Sarina groaned. "It's like taking a third wheel, or in this case a fifth wheel. My friends don't want my little brothers hanging around. It's not like I'm a weanling. I can take care of myself, you know."

"Not on your life, darling. Take Jason, Wade, or Joshua, but you don't step out of this house alone."

His blue eyes, so unlike hers, brooked absolutely no argument. Sighing loud enough to convey her irritation, Sarina agreed. "Fine. I'll take Joshua."

"Good," Romeo said with a nod of finality. "When are you leaving?"

"About an hour. I guess I'll go ask him if he'd mind accompanying me."

"Sounds good. Have a good time."

As she walked out, Sarina heard her mother say, "You can't keep her trapped forever. Sooner or later she'll either find the exit, or make one."

"That's what scares me," her father replied.

Chapter Three

Brody arrived at their meeting place with a smile on his face. Standing before him was a beautiful woman in a dress that screamed sexy. "I have to come up with a word better than amazing but you, sweetheart, look amazing."

"Thank you," Sarina smiled. "Just in case you need them; phenomenal, gorgeous, and stunning all work as well."

"I'll keep that in mind," Brody grinned. "How'd you ditch your chaperone?"

"I chose my youngest brother and gave him two hundred dollars to get lost."

"And smart as hell too. Very nice."

"Wanna go for a walk?"

"Absolutely," Brody said, offering his hand. She took it readily and Brody pulled her a little closer. "Would it bother you if we talked about some personal things?"

"No, what would you like to know?"

"Anything you want to tell me."

"Okay," she smiled. "I'm the oldest of five. I have a twin named Jason, then Wade is in the middle and Shawna and Joshua, who are also twins, make up the end."

"Wow, your parents really got busy didn't they?" Brody chuckled when Sarina blushed. "Is sex an uncomfortable topic for you?"

"Not uncomfortable, just… I don't have a lot, if any, experience to draw on so I usually avoid the topic altogether."

"Ah," Brody smiled. "We can fix that you know."

"Fix what?" Sarina asked.

"Your experience. Sex is certainly something to be enjoyed, breeding season or not."

"Brody," Sarina blushed. "We can't just… we barely know each other."

"Not true," he laughed. "I know that you hate seafood as you barely touched your plate last night. You like to wear your hair up, but don't mind having it down either. You love your family, but feel smothered by them. You dress nicely, but not extravagantly, which tells me you're not a showy sort of person. You're private about your life and it embarrasses you a little to be the center of attention."

"How do you—"

"And," Brody grinned, stopping so that she'd face him. "You like kissing me."

"Well I can't exactly deny that."

"Good," he said, his stormy eyes locking with her dark ones. There was a breath of hesitation before he took her mouth. Their first kiss had been heated by his need. Now that he'd chained that need inside him, he could now give her only sweetness. Slowly he covered her lips with his own, tasting the need and hunger that mixed with her flavor. Lust, hot and heavy, swam through his system as his own desire made itself known.

"Do you know how good you feel, how good you taste?"

"I've waited my whole life for this," Sarina breathed.

"Then let me have you. There's no better place than one we make for ourselves."

"I can't," she said, stepping back. "My parents would kill me."

"You just said you've waited your whole life for this. Why do you think that is?"

"Because… because I wasn't ready before now."

"Okay," Brody said, slowing down. "You weren't ready before, which means you are ready now. I'd venture a guess that you hadn't found the right man until now either. How many times did your parents parade you around like a prized cow?"

"How did you—"

"You're an alpha's daughter, my sweet girl. It's expected for an alpha male to show off his eldest daughter. You'll be the first of his line to come into breeding season."

"As I grew older he did it more frequently, until this year. I asked him to let me choose for myself the mate I want."

"And what did your dear old dad say?"

"That it was my choice as long as he approved."

"Then it's not really your choice, is it?"

Sarina didn't like admitting that Brody had a point. Could it really be her choice if her father had the final say?

"I'm not asking you to do anything you don't want to, sweetheart," Brody assured her. "I'm just asking you to be honest with me and yourself."

"I don't know anything about pleasing you. What if I mess up?"

"That's the lovely thing. As long as you're willing, you can't mess up."

Sarina wasn't so sure about that, but Brody was standing there looking so damn sexy with his dark hair just long enough to give his sharp edged jaw a dangerous look. His blue eyes were full of impatient need. Sarina had known from the moment she'd seen him that Brody Duscene would be an important part of her life. If this wasn't it, then why did she want him so bad? Her mother had always told her she'd know when it was right. This, being with Brody, certainly didn't feel wrong.

"I don't think—"

"Good," Brody cut her off. Then his mouth was on hers again, this time showing her the hunger in him. His hands ran up her thighs as he picked her up and carried her to a part of the pasture that was overgrown. Suddenly the soft grass was beneath her and Brody knelt beside her. "I want you begging for me."

"I can't even get my bearings," Sarina said, sitting up. "There's so much going on inside my body."

"You have no idea, darling," Brody grinned. He leaned over to kiss her and ran a hand up her thigh again as he laid her back. "I want you Sarina, in a way I've never wanted another woman. I want every inch of you to scream for me."

"But how do I—"

"Just let me touch you, taste you. The more you do that, the better it'll be for both of us."

"Alright," she agreed, as his hand slid between her legs. Fire raced through her system when Brody slipped into her wet pussy. Her breath came short as Sarina tried to harness the overwhelming feelings that Brody's touch evoked in her. The need to know and understand had her own hands touching in turn, feeling the warm flesh beneath her fingers. Within minutes their outer clothes were gone and Sarina lay in the grass in less than she'd wear to the beach.

"Oh God, let me taste you Sarina," Brody begged, his cock already hard and ready.

"Don't most men already want to get on with things?"

"I'm not like most men, darling. I want to feast on you, especially your first time. I do hope though that we'll have plenty more times like this."

Sarina looked up into those dark, needy eyes and felt her entire world shift. Yesterday, Brody was nothing more than a nice guy who'd asked her to dinner. Now he was the man who possessed the qualities she wanted in a mate. "Do we mate now?"

"No," Brody choked out a laugh. "It's not usually customary to mate when it's a woman's first time. It can be painful to some and adding mating to it can be less than satisfactory."

"Oh," Sarina said, disappointed.

Brody tipped her face up and smiled. "Just enjoy today with me. Mating time will come soon enough when we're ready."

"So you want to mate with me?"

"I wouldn't have asked you out if the intention was just pleasure. Nor would I be this patient. Someday I may waive my patience and take you hard and fast against a wall somewhere. But today, I want to experience every moment of your first time."

"You'll be gentle?"

Oh, this woman, Brody thought, resting his brow against hers. Lifting his head after a minute he pressed a kiss there. "I will treat you with the utmost care and respect, Sarina. You are an alpha's daughter and deserving of every consideration."

Brody watched her whole demeanor change right before his eyes. Gone was the timid and shy girl. Here now was the confident seductress. Sitting up she grabbed his hands and put them over her breasts, looking up into his face. Her dark eyes were nearly black with passion and a need to know. "Then teach me, won't you?"

Brody watched as Sarina unclasped her bra, letting it fall away to expose the prettiest breasts he'd ever seen. One even had a tiny mole that his lips wanted to kiss. If he was going to teach her, then he'd teach her what he loved about her, starting with her perfect body. He trailed hot, wet kisses over her flesh, igniting a fire inside her that he hoped would rage for days on end. His hands roamed over the places his mouth touched, and brought her to climax easily. When she was breathlessly begging for more, he brought her hand to him, to show her how aroused she made him. "This is what you do to me sweetheart," he said, running her warm palm against his hardened shaft.

This time when she lay down, Brody covered her, settling himself between her thighs. When his tip touched her wet slit he groaned, holding himself back. Biting back his own need, Brody waited, testing her. He was ripe for sure, but it wasn't until she reached for him that he knew she was also ready and willing. "Mate with me Brody."

"Sarina," he breathed. "I don't—"

"I've never wanted anyone as I do you. As an alpha's daughter, I was always raised to know myself, what I wanted, what I would and wouldn't settle for. I want you as my mate and nothing I say or do, nothing you say or do is going to change that. So why shouldn't it be today at a moment that's special to us both?"

Moved beyond measure, Brody sighed and pressed his brow to hers again. "You're sure?"

"I am," she grinned, one side of her mouth tilting up before the other. He kissed her then, pressing his tip into her wet folds.

"Then breathe for me and when we finish, we need to bite each other. From today on, you won't want any other male, nor will I take any other female. You understand how permanent this is?"

"I do," Sarina said. Her dark eyes were focused, alert, and very serious. Brody pressed against her before he drew out. Watching the expectation on her face, Brody waited until her body relaxed and then he pierced her, joining their bodies in a love they were both just discovering. Slowly he moved inside her hot pussy, letting her body adjust to the fullness of his thick cock. Slowly she started to move with him as the pain in her eyes ebbed away. Her hands found his flesh and touched him everywhere. Her wet tongue flicked over his tight nipple, making him jump. "Do men not like that?"

"Not many of them," he said. "It's more the woman who tends to like that particular attention."

"Oh," she said. He kissed her then, drawing out her sweetness.

"Learning is never a bad thing, Sarina," he encouraged. "How can you know what I like if you don't try?"

Pressing into her again, Brody kissed her, sliding his tongue back and forth with the rhythm he set inside her. Slowly he pulled out and pressed into her, feeling the tight press of her swollen folds. Soon their bodies were beyond verbal communication and the talking became moans and low growls of pleasure. Brody built her up, wanting her first time to be something she'd never forget.

He touched her thighs and hips, ran his hands up to cup and knead her breasts, twisting their tight, pink tips between his fingers. Then he felt her body tighten sporadically around him, growing in strength. Pulling back his own need, Brody waited as he thrust into her over and over again, teasing her with shallow thrusts that were alternated by deeply piercing jabs. Only when her body started to pulse with his rhythm did Brody think about his own wants. Soon he pushed her over, knowing he'd follow soon behind.

"God yes, Sarina," he groaned. And as their orgasm swept them off, Sarina felt Brody's sharp canines sink into the supple flesh of her neck where it met her collarbone. Her first reaction was a gasp before her own teeth pierced him. The heavy taste of iron mixed with his scent filled her senses so that she was overwhelmed by him. When the orgasm passed, Sarina felt her teeth retract and sat back heavily, blood still dripping from her lips. She looked up at Brody, noting the four puncture wounds on his neck.

"I can smell you, like you're inside me."

"It'll be like that, strong and overpowering. Then you'll get used to it."

"Will I know where you are, how you are?"

"I've heard some tell that once two wolves are mated, they never have a moment's peace again, so I'd say it's likely that we'll know where and how the other is, yes."

"I want to be with you again," Sarina said, a blush covering her skin.

"Too much more and you won't be able to walk tomorrow."

"Is that a bad thing?"

"It will be if your dad finds out what we've done."

"My dad isn't that old school."

"Oh yeah?" Brody laughed. "By all means then, why not go home and show him your mating mark. I bet he'll be real happy to learn that his eldest daughter, who's officially in season now, will be forever tied to the likes of me."

"What the hell's that supposed to mean?"

"It means, sweetheart, that I will love and care for you to the absolute best of my ability for the rest of eternity. And that your dad is going to hate me for at least that long."

"My dad won't hate you," Sarina chuckled. She eventually said farewell to Brody with a promise to see him the following day and she straightened out her clothes and headed home. She wasn't within five hundred feet of her home when Jason came running out to her.

"Word to the wise. Stay away from Dad. He is beyond pissed at you."

"Why?"

"Really, you're going to ask me that when you know damn well why he's peeved. He and Mom ran into Joshua in town. He was all too happy to tell them that you'd given him money to get lost. Twenty-four or not, I wouldn't want Dad that mad at me. And why do you smell like a mangy dog?"

"I do not smell like a mangy—"

"Sarina Mabel, you get your ass in this house this instant," Romeo said, his words nearly a growl from the front porch.

Sarina followed Jason who had the most sympathetic look on his face. It was when she stepped up to her father though, that Romeo's eyes went wide with shock. "Oh Christ, tell me you didn't!" Before she could evade him, his arm caught her wrist and his hand pulled back the neckline of her dress, clearly exposing four puncture wounds on her neck. "Son-of-a-bitch, Sarina!"

The growl that emanated from her father nearly had her trembling in her heels and brought every member of their family into the family room. Sarina felt the hot press of embarrassment singe her cheeks as her siblings looked on in shock. Anger and disappointment raced each other through her body, anger finally winning out. Lashing out, she shared it with her father in equal portion.

"Don't you sit there and pretend like you're so noble. We all know how you were with Mom when she'd barely even known what a werewolf was, let alone that she was one. I've known my whole life, have waited my whole life. I'm a grown woman, whether anyone in this house wants to admit it or not."

"You'll watch your tone in this house!" Romeo said, drawing strength from Amanda who came to stand beside him. The hurt in her mother's eyes did little to stem her frustration.

"I'm tired of doing as I'm told without any explanation as to why. The man I love will forever be mine now and I will be his. I'm not ashamed of that fact, nor am I ashamed of my having been with him. You can all look at me as if you're holier-than-thou with your pious, shitty attitudes. I don't care what anyone in this house or any other thinks. I know Brody Duscene and he knows me and loves me!"

Without another word, Sarina turned and rushed upstairs, slamming her door for emphasis.

Chapter Four

"You may all be excused," Romeo said, holding onto Amanda's hand. "And I want absolute silence on this issue until I say otherwise."

"What do we do now?" Amanda asked.

"We find out everything we can about Brody Duscene," Romeo said. "Can you locate him?"

"Of course," Amanda said, but added, "I do, however, feel it's a slight betrayal of our daughter's trust."

"She just destroyed our trust in her."

"I was talking more of her trust in us," Amanda smiled. "We've always been open and honest with her and the other children. Whether you like it or not, darling, our daughter is grown. She's free to love and be loved in return, to choose a mate."

"She hasn't even brought him home, Amanda," Romeo groaned.

"I'm not sure I would have brought you home, either, had my father been alive and acted as you just did."

"So I should have just acted like nothing happened?"

"That's not what I'm saying. You could have done it a little more privately. You humiliated her for following her heart, something I've always told our children to do."

"That was before their heart led them to do stupid, reckless things. As far as I know, there is no Brody Duscene in our pack and that worries me."

"Regardless, love, we have to fix this. I won't see our family fall apart because our daughter fell in love."

"You do realize that she'll go into season with the full moon don't you?"

"Yes," Amanda grinned. "Are we too young to be Papa and Nana?"

"Ugh," Romeo groaned, making Amanda laugh.

After things had calmed down some, Amanda made two cups of hot chocolate and carried them on a tray up to Sarina's room. She knocked twice and with no answer gently pushed the unlocked door open. "Sarina?"

When no answer came forth, Amanda set the tray down and searched the room, quickly realizing that Sarina was nowhere to be found. "Romeo!"

"What is it?" he asked, bounding up the stairs three at a time. Coming to the same conclusion as his wife, he called for his three sons to start looking around the property. "Does anyone know where this Brody Duscene lives?" With no forthcoming information, Romeo called his entire family to meet him at the house for further details.

"What do we know so far?" Elijah asked, holding his wife's, Penelope's, hand. As a wind Radiant, Penelope could invoke everything from a cool breeze to a tornado at the drop of a hat. It was something she had to learn to control while Amanda was learning to harness the power of the Earth. Only when Amanda had become their leader did the Radiants have free rein to marry whom they deemed worthy. Thanks to Amanda's rational thinking, Penelope and Elijah were finally able to acknowledge their love for one another.

"Not much I'm afraid," Romeo said to his younger brother. "Brody Duscene is the wolf we're looking for. He's not of our pack and we have no real details on him. You should also be aware that he is Sarina's mate." An audible gasp that swept through the entire group was exactly how Romeo still felt.

"And you think she went to him?" Jeremiah asked. As Romeo's father and the father of his deceased twin, Damon, he had once been the alpha of their great pack. His hair now going white and his eyes a dimmer blue than they once were, he still stood as a great leader in their pack and Romeo couldn't come close to adequately expressing the love and respect he had for his father.

"I have no doubt of it. She's covered in his scent and the musk of new love. She would scarcely run anywhere else."

"You know, if she has gone to him, there's no real way you can make her come back." This came from Romeo's youngest sister, Audri, who was as outspoken as his own daughter.

"Yes," Romeo replied. He was thankful when Benjamin stepped up and put an arm around Audri's waist. How she had gotten herself a man like Benjamin, Romeo would never know. He was the perfect balance of calm and rationale for his high strung sister.

"We need to know she's safe," Audri's twin, Aurora, said. Her husband, James, who'd come along well after Amanda had given birth to Wade, was sitting next to her on the couch. "Whether or not she comes home at this point isn't really the problem."

"What?" Romeo said rather pointedly.

"I was just trying to point out that Sarina is grown now, whether anyone in the family likes it or not. She's also of breeding age, Gramps," retorted Audri.

Romeo let the dig slide as everyone chuckled. "Just wait until your Katie is there, dear sister of mine. Then we'll see how funny you think it is."

"She's got at least five years, big brother."

"They'll fly by," he said with a note of obvious sadness in his voice.

"Alright," Jeremiah said, taking over. He wasn't the alpha any longer, but his family respected him and gave him leave. "Let's split up in two's, no less than two couples per quadrant. I want my granddaughter and her mate found."

The family did as he asked. Aurora and Audri took the north quadrant with their husbands. Elijah and Penelope agreed to take the west quadrant with Sebastian and Bryce, two of Romeo's younger brothers and Sebastian's wife, Lacie. Romeo's other brother, Joseph, and his wife, Rachel, agreed to take the south quadrant with Romeo and Amanda. "And I'll take the east quadrant with the grandchildren – all of them," Jeremiah said, his statement final.

The search began in earnest as the moon began to rise higher in the sky. Sarina's entire family branched out, hoping to find her safe and sound by morning. It'd be a difficult search, stretching into territory that was beyond the borders of their community and putting Romeo and Amanda, the reigning King and Queen, in a very delicate situation.

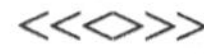

Sarina swiped at the angry tears that poured from her eyes as her soul oozed out its heartache. She'd always believed that her parents loved her, wanted her. She'd always seen them as strict, but fair. Now all those visions were nothing but ash. She tossed them to the wind as she ran, sobbing through the woods. Using the power inside her, she reached out to Brody, willing him to answer her.

Her power poured from the pain in her heart, making her chest ache as she left behind her family to reach for the man she loved. She couldn't explain it, but her mother had been right. She'd waited her whole life for the man she'd love into eternity and it had struck her like a lightning bolt when Brody had shown up in her life. Newly mated or not, she'd known him from the moment he'd spoken to her.

"What's a pretty little thing like you doing out so late?" came a surly voice. Sarina used her keen vision to spot the man, who looked to be three sheets to the wind, with a bottle of rum in his hand.

"I like late night walks."

"Me too," the man chuckled. "Especially when a pretty woman happens by. You got a name, sugar?"

"I do, as my parents saw fit to give me one when I was born."

"Funny," he said, his voice hardening. "You going to tell me what it is?"

"No," Sarina said, bunching her muscles tight. If she had to, she'd turn and try shift to save herself. The moon wasn't full yet and she'd never changed before. From what she learned from the pack, the pain would be beyond anything she'd ever endured, but if it meant saving her life, she'd do it. "And trust me when I tell you, you don't want to push me on that one."

"Oh?" he laughed cynically.

"Please sir, just enjoy your rum and leave me to what I was doing."

"What were you doing, darling? Because from here it looked like a whole lot of nothing. Now, you and me on the other hand, we could spend some late night time enjoying the more carnal aspects of our anatomy. I'd even share my rum with you if you want a nip."

"No, thank you," Sarina said. She watched the man's eyes go steel hard and turned to run when his hand caught her hair, yanking her viciously backward. She landed hard on her back, feeling the crunch of rocks under her skin. The man, who moved much faster than she'd given him credit for, considering his inebriated state, was on top of her in seconds, his hands roughly pushing and pulling at her clothes. Her scream hit the air like a gunshot until the back of his hand landed across her cheek. The sting stole her breath and his weight prevented her from drawing another deep breath to try again.

"I like a feisty woman," the man chuckled. "Makes the taking so much more fun. You ever have a man inside you, baby?"

Sarina nearly vomited from the stench of his breath as his mouth landed on her neck. Still sore from where Brody had marked her, Sarina's eyes watered from the man's harsh mouth. Slowly she drew in her breath and screamed again, unable to find the energy to shift with his weight crushing her. Suddenly Sarina heard a feral growl and the man was lifted off of her, his body slamming into a rock. Sarina would have sat up and moved, except for the huge, nearly jet black wolf that stood protectively over her, his face pinned on the man.

"What the hell?" the man said, rubbing his sore head. "Got yourself a pet, do you darling? Well a bullet should take care of him! Then you and I can get back to a little—" Sarina watched as the wolf tore the man's throat out, leaving his body as it fell. When he walked back to her, Sarina touched his coat, her hand gliding over the silky fur.

"Brody?" she asked, looking into the wolf's golden eyes. Licking his muzzle clean, the wolf sat down close to her and yelped as his body shifted back to human form. Seeing that it was Brody, Sarina stripped her shirt off and covered him with it. She stroked his shaggy hair as he finished the change. "You found me."

Brody finally sat up, catching his breath after the change. Knowing the man in him wouldn't get there in time, he'd changed on the run and the wolf had taken over. He hadn't known it was in him to change until he'd heard Sarina scream. He'd never even heard of anyone but an alpha being able to change before the full moon, until now. "I heard you screaming," Brody explained. "Before that, I was sure I heard you in my head. You were crying."

"I was sad and angry," Sarina said, the same feelings still inside her.

"Your parents are angry huh?"

"My dad acted as if he hadn't forced my mother to marry him. She may have made the decision willingly, but not before he practically bashed her over the head with all of it. And he has the audacity to sit there and act as if I've made some terrible decision."

"Then come home with me."

"You want me to leave my pack?"

"I just want you safe, Sarina. And I'd like to put on clothes that are actually made for a man's body."

Giggling, Sarina's eyes danced. "I can't talk you out of that, huh?"

Brody chuckled, "I didn't know my mate had such a thing for nature."

"We're werewolves, Brody. It's sort of half of what we do."

"True," he grinned. Pulling her close, Brody took her mouth, falling into her. As it always seemed to, her flavor punched through his system, warming all the cold places as her hands touched him. Passion, ignited by love, flamed through them both, burning its way to the surface so that everywhere she touched grew hot and hard. Within minutes Brody didn't care that he was naked as a jaybird in the middle of the forest at twilight. All he knew was that the only woman he wanted, wanted him just as desperately.

<<◇>>

"Can you find them?" Romeo asked as he and Amanda set out with Joseph and Rachel.

"It'd be better if I had something that belonged to him, but having his scent on her clothing will work." Amanda stepped away from her husband with Sarina's dress in her hands. Lifting her hands high in the air she called on the Earth to give up what it held. "Powers of Earth hear my call. Give up the blood you hold in thrall. Track my daughter wherever she might go. Find her mate as well, great spirit, as I will, so mote it be."

Romeo watched as a small trail of Earth spewed up from the ground, lit by a white glow. It headed west where Penelope, Elijah, Bryce, Sebastian and Lacie were looking. "Will they know what they're looking at?"

"Penelope will know," Amanda assured him.

"Let's head that way then."

It took nearly an hour for Romeo and Amanda, Joseph and Rachel to reach the others. By then Jeremiah was on his way with the older grandchildren, as were Audri and Aurora with their mates.

"What do we know?" Audri asked, voicing everyone's thoughts.

"We definitely know they're in this quadrant, but well outside our community as the trail died off here," Penelope said, pointing toward a forest of trees.

"Should we spread out?" Elijah asked, looking to Amanda and Romeo.

"No," he said. "Can you and Penelope take the kids and Dad back to the house? Joseph, Bryce, Sebastian, Audri and Aurora will help us search."

"Alright," Elijah agreed. After they'd headed back into the safety of their community, Romeo and Amanda headed into the woods, straight on from where the trail left off. Just out of eyesight, Aurora and Audri, along with their husbands, took the left section and Joseph and Sebastian, with their wives and Bryce took the right section.

The woods were thick, mainly with birch and oak trees that grew tall and beautiful to block out both the sun and the moon. Even with their keen eyesight, the eleven werewolves had a hard time seeing, until Amanda did a quick chant. Turning toward his wife, Romeo smiled. "Thanks," he smiled. "Who knew owls could see so keenly?"

"Well they do hunt at night," Amanda felt the need to point out. "Now put them to use and find our girl."

Twenty minutes later Sebastian came running toward them. "There's a large cave over here that looks feasible for a pack if it's small enough." The four of them checked it out and found no evidence of a wolf pack using the space.

"Keep looking," Romeo said, moving back toward the center with Amanda.

Over the next half an hour no one saw anything remotely useable for a wolf pack of any size, until Romeo saw a massive cave. "Amanda," he whispered.

"I see it. But how do we alert Sebastian and the others?"

"Can you signal them with a spell?"

"I could try astral projection," Amanda said, already preparing. Centering herself she chanted what always sounded like nonsense to Romeo. Thankfully she was a truly talented Radiant witch with excellent and very honed knowledge. He saw an instant flash and then it was as if Amanda stood stock still, almost as if she'd been turned to stone like a victim of Medusa. In a moment she was back to herself, a smile spreading across her face. "That was fairly amazing."

"Excellent hon, now we need a plan."

Sarina took in the expanse of the cave walls, shuddering as the damp cold sank into her bones. "It's freezing in here."

"I'll build a fire once we get to my room."

"Why do you all live in a cave?"

"It's actually a set of caves that run through this side of Mount Chastain. It's well networked and gives our pack plenty of room to spread out without tripping over each other."

"There are some, most in fact, in your pack that don't like me here."

"They just need to get to know you."

"Brody I'm not so sure—"

"What is she doing here?"

Sarina took shelter behind Brody's strong back as he stood up taller, obviously addressing the alpha of his pack. "She is my mate and when she was turned out of her parents' home for being with me, I brought her to the safety of my home."

"She doesn't belong here, Brody."

"Regardless of how you feel about her, she's staying."

"Then I want both of you out," Reggie said, turning his back on Brody.

"We can't travel tonight. We'll be gone first thing in the morning if that's what you want."

"I don't care when you go, but she doesn't sleep or stay another moment in the presence of our pack. Her coward of a father doesn't deserve the New Delta Community. If she even knew what he'd done, along with his father, she'd think twice about claiming her parentage. Not to mention that whore of a mother of hers."

Sarina growled low in her throat and stepped out from behind Brody, her eyes gleaming as she faced him. "You have no right to speak of my family that way. Who are you to pass judgement? You have your meager pack hiding out in a dank cave."

Sarina saw the punishment coming and ducked to avoid it. What she wasn't fast enough to avoid was the silver bullet that slammed into her shoulder. It seeped into her system and kept her wolf from emerging. "Now, Lady Traverse, you might want to think twice about your decisions from here on out. This next bullet won't be so nice."

Sarina looked up to see Reggie pointing a revolver at Brody's head. Wincing, she stood up slowly. "I'll leave, right now." Brody caught her hand, imploring her to stay.

"You can meet me when you're ready," Sarina said, leaning up to kiss him, "I'll be waiting." Stepping outside the entrance of the cave, Sarina breathed in the fresh air, thankful she was no longer inside the wet and cold cave. Bullet in her shoulder or not, she felt sorry for the wolves that lived under Reggie's regime. He seemed to be a classless leader who demanded obedience instead of earning his wolves' respect.

"Sarina?" She turned at the sound of her mother's voice.

"Mama? What are you doing here?"

"We've had the whole family out looking for you, darling. Your father is just as hard-headed and stubborn as you are. That doesn't mean that you have to run away."

"I won't let Brody go just to please Daddy, Mama."

"No one's asking you to let him go. We just want to get to know him. We want a chance to see what you see in him."

"We need to find a place to settle first," Sarina said, her body giving in to the silver that was still oozing into her bloodstream. Taking a labored breath she continued. "We can come visit once we get settled, but I can't go back home. Finding Brody helped me realize that I need my own life. I can't live the life Dad or you want for me anymore."

"Alright," Amanda replied. Her eyes went wide as she saw the blood seeping out of Sarina's wound. "You're hurt."

Sarina felt as if her body weighed a ton as she took a step toward her mother. Then the world went black.

Chapter Five

"Romeo!" Amanda called as she held Sarina in her arms.

"Sarina!" Romeo called out, tapping his daughter's cheeks. "Come on sweetheart." Amanda pulled back Sarina's hair, noticing the silver nitrate that coated her damp locks.

"It's silver," Amanda choked.

"We need to get her home. Hold onto her, Amanda. I'll change and run her home."

"Wait," came a voice from behind them. Amanda turned to see a handsome young man approach them. "Let me take her, please."

"You must be Brody," Amanda said, a motherly smile on her face.

"I'm Brody Duscene and it's awfully nice to meet you, Mrs. Traverse. I can see where Sarina gets her good looks."

"Flattery only gets you so far, son."

Brody grinned and stepped up to Romeo.

"I know that we have a lot to talk about, but your daughter's welfare is just as much my responsibility as yours. More so now that we've mated. Please let me take her home."

"You can't move as fast as I can. I can change before the full moon."

Brody gave Romeo what could only be called a cocky wink and then with a loud yelp of pain changed into his wolf, rubbing his nose against Sarina's hand.

"Well, shit," exclaimed Romeo.

"We can't stand here all night, Romeo," Amanda said. "Let's get everyone home and get Sarina comfortable before we talk anymore."

"I don't know how to let her go," Romeo said, touching his daughter's head. Grown or not, she was still that little girl who'd climbed onto his lap in her fluffy pajamas begging for a story or anything that would get her extra time before she had to go to bed.

"Then for right now, let's just let Brody take her home. We'll be right behind him and we can take better care of her there than standing out here in the middle of nowhere."

Romeo helped Amanda secure Sarina's limp body to Brody's back and then gave a solemn nod that had Brody leaping through the forest like the wind. "He's a mite faster than me," Romeo said, the first signs of a grin on his face. "Maybe our girl didn't choose so terribly after all."

"She loves him," Amanda said simply. "That much I know."

"How?"

"The way she looks when she talks about him, as I did you not so long ago. I like to think I still look at you that way."

<<◇>>

Brody bounded up the steps of the Traverse home and scratched the door, whining a howl as he did.

"Well look at you," Jeremiah Traverse said, "Come in and bring our girl. Elijah can you help this pup with Sarina?"

Brody sat patiently, waiting for Elijah to lift Sarina from his back. The change came over him in an instant, his body exhausted and unable to hold its wolf any longer. He collapsed to the floor in a heap of tired, naked man. Female giggles erupted from the stairwell and Jeremiah cussed. Brody barely felt the sheet cover him before he was crawling over to Sarina. Resting his forehead against hers, he whispered to her, "Come on love. You're home now. We can't have you lying about. We've got plans, remember? I need you with me Sarina. I can't do this without you."

"Who did this to her?" Romeo asked. Brody could tell by the way the front door slammed shut that Romeo Traverse was pissed and for good reason. Tucking the sheet around him, he stood up. Facing an alpha was hard enough. Facing your mate's father, who was also an alpha was nearly impossible.

"My alpha did, sir. Reggie is careless, especially where your pack in concerned. He's convinced that he should rule the entire Delta area. He said that your father took this portion of the pack unethically."

"Reginald Baxter," Jeremiah said, his voice still booming for his age, "is nothing more than a lowlife sleaze who just happened to come from the same genes as all wolves. Fenris," he continued, "was a philanderer. Something that didn't pass Lilith's attention. It was exactly what she had planned all along. The more women Fenris slept with, the more wolves there would be. She knew eventually she'd come across a male who burned her blood and ruled with the tenacity you exhibited, Romeo. It was why she did as she pleased. She didn't care about Damon or any other wolf, until you. She wanted to rule as Queen and it was you that stirred her. Fenris, however, was turned on by nearly any female figure that passed in front of his eyes. When Reginald's mother came to the Delta, we tried to take her in, much like your father, Amanda. Lilith would not hear of it though and made sure that Reginald would not only rule his own pack, but would turn to the dark magic as well."

"What was her end game?" Brody asked.

"She was delusional by the time we dealt death to her," said Romeo.

"I'm afraid she was always that disturbed," Jeremiah said, hanging his head in sadness. "It is my great shame that I could not save my son from her wiles."

"Damon chose his own path, Father," Romeo said. "It still doesn't answer why Reggie shot Sarina with a silver bullet."

"She challenged him," Brody said. "Before I could stop her, she stepped out from behind me and challenged Reggie. He shot her because she was standing up for you, her family."

"And you let him?" Elijah asked, his eyes hard as granite. "You just stood there and let him shoot her?"

"I didn't see the gun until he'd already pulled the trigger and by then he'd pointed it at my head. If I'd moved an inch I'd be dead and so would she," Brody said, standing to his full height, easily six inches over Elijah.

"You have the makings of an alpha, son."

"My father was the leader of the Hemstead Basin before he was murdered. Reggie found me and took me in, but I didn't realize until recently where my bloodline came from. I would have become the alpha of that pack one day, had my father lived."

"How was he murdered?"

"Lilith," Brody said. "Only he called her Delilah. He spoke of her incessantly, like she was a drug inside his system. He couldn't get over her. She asked him to meet her one day and I begged him not to go. I followed him and watched as she slept with him. Then she pulled out a revolver and shot him in the head with a silver bullet. The alpha passed to my father's brother, Rueben. He took a sweet woman as his mate and they've ruled the Hemstead Basin together ever since."

"Why didn't you go home?"

"When Reggie found me I was incoherent, inconsolable. It took them months to get me to talk in any sort of manner that would pass as communication. Three years later I was able to start leading, but by then I figured anyone who would have attempted to look for me probably figured I was dead, so I became dead to them and them to me. After that I never tried to go back."

"Do you wish to lead now?"

"I won't take an alpha position I haven't earned and I won't jeopardize Sarina for it."

"Good," Romeo said.

They talked well into the morning as Amanda tended to their daughter.

"How is she?" Brody asked, concerned.

"She'll heal, thankfully."

"May I see her?"

"She's in her room," Amanda smiled. "First door on the left, top of the stairs." Brody nodded and made his way up the winding staircase.

"Sarina?" he said, knocking softly on the door. Stepping into the quiet room he saw her lying on the bed, her body covered by a thick comforter. A diffuser was set up with a strength potion to help her regain what she'd lost.

"Hi handsome," she smiled. Brody took her hand as she reached out to him and gently sat on the side of the bed. "I missed you while I was sleeping."

"I never knew I could worry so much, or miss you so much," Brody sighed. He lay down with her, certain not to jostle her weakened body.

"You're darn right you'd better miss me," she said, smiling. Brody turned toward her, marveling at her beauty. Even after being shot and nearly succumbing to the silver in her system, she was exquisite. Giving into the need, he leaned over and kissed her. The sweetness of her slow offering eased the ache in his soul. Then her hands came up to cup his face and she looked deep into his eyes.

"Sarina," Brody breathed. Resting his brow on hers his eyes looked into hers. "You have to rest. I can't touch you when you were next to dying just moments ago."

"Then lie down and sleep with me some. Your presence is the balm my soul needs."

Brody wrapped a protective arm around Sarina and drew her gently to him before they both fell asleep.

<<<>>>

"How's she doing?" asked Romeo

"As good as can be expected. It'll take her a couple of days to regain her footing. Having Brody here should help," said Amanda.

"Where is the little whelp?"

"I sent him up to see her. I believe they're sleeping, which will do them both a world of good."

"I just can't get over it, Amanda. She's our daughter. We raised her to always come to us, to trust us. How could she hide this from us?"

"I don't think she did hide it, love. I just think it overwhelmed her. If my instincts are right, she didn't intend to mate with Brody. It was as spontaneous as the change the first time it happens."

"But we taught her to be open and honest with us. Then all of a sudden she turns twenty-four and she's mated within days of her first breeding season? I didn't even know she was interested in anyone."

"No one did," Amanda said. "I'm not sure they knew each other long before this all happened."

"And look how that turned out," Romeo grumbled.

"Pot," Amanda grinned and pointed toward the ceiling, "kettle. You can't have forgotten that our own meeting and mating wasn't nearly as smooth as a baby's bottom."

"This is different," he sighed. He obviously wasn't fooling his wife. Had she always seen right through him like that? "So what do we do now?"

"Right now," Amanda said, grinning in that way that always turned him on, "we tell everyone who doesn't live here, to go home and rest. We let Sarina and Brody rest."

"What about us?"

"I think we can find something better than rest to occupy our thoughts and time."

Romeo chuckled. She was a woman after his own heart if he'd ever known one. It took them nearly an hour to get everyone out and get their other children to various parts of the house. Romeo, knowing full well that their children would grow up someday, had made sure that the only bedroom downstairs was his and Amanda's. He'd also had it outfitted with soundproof walls and a solid door that didn't let much escape. Taking his wife's hand, he led her down the hallway, turning toward the staircase.

"I just want to check on her," he said. When Amanda pulled him back though, he sighed.

"Trust," she said patiently, "starts now."

"How'd you become the wise one?"

"Oh honey," Amanda laughed, "I've always been the wise one. In the beginning I just hid it better so I wouldn't bruise your ego."

Pulling her into their room, Romeo took her mouth with a fervor that never seemed to dim for her. Her long, slender arms came around his neck as she sank into him. Turning, Romeo walked her, giggling, toward their bed. She laid down willingly… something she'd done from the very beginning. It humbled him to know that even after twenty-four years of marriage and scarcely more than that of being together, she was still leading him. It didn't take a rocket scientist to see that he was the one who'd been blessed by her and not the other way around. Did all women affect their men in that way?

Grinning, Romeo stripped his shirt off and plopped down next to her, smiling when she turned toward him, laughing. Cupping her cheek, he ran his thumb over her full mouth, marveling at her beauty. Drawing her to him, Romeo kissed her soundly, sinking into everything he loved about her.

Sarina woke the next morning feeling as if someone had weighed her body down by injecting sand into her veins. She knew it was the effects of the silver wearing off, but it didn't help. Every time she tried to move it was like trudging through tar. Brody stirred beside her and resettled, still sleeping soundly. She managed to make it to the shower and felt ten times better when she emerged. When she opened the bedroom door, Brody was on the other side, waiting.

"You scared me," she breathed, smiling.

"Don't leave, okay?"

"I still have to dress as I haven't streaked in front of my family since the age of two or three."

"Good," Brody smiled.

Sarina pulled her towel tighter and turned toward her closet, rifling through it as Brody closed the bathroom door. Brody was back out in minutes, his strong arms wrapping around her middle. "You smell good," he cooed.

"I feel pretty good," Sarina smiled, turning in his arms so she could see his face. She'd known from the beginning that it was his eyes, those beautiful pair of baby blues that could be light as glass or dark as a good storm that had drawn her in. She was thankful all over again that she'd picked him. "Kiss me, won't you?"

He smiled and Sarina let him draw her down to her bed. Sitting on his lap she realized that love, the kind that grips your heart in a choke hold and never lets go, had snuck in when she hadn't been expecting it.

"I love you, Brody," she said, watching his eyes change from that light beauty to the raging storm. It was so damned sexy when he did that. "You don't have to say it back, I just—"

His lips claimed hers in a rush of heat that scorched her soul. Passion like she'd never known swamped her as his hands tore her towel away, exposing the pink, naked flesh beneath. Instantly her breasts tightened at his touch, and his mouth found them irresistible. Sarina's head fell back as Brody's warm tongue slid hot and wet over first one nipple and then the other. Ignited in a way no one had ever made her feel before him, Sarina let the fog descend over her, pushing out everything and everyone, but the wonderful man who was with her in this moment.

Her hands found the button to his jeans and undid it, pulling those denim pants down past his knees. He kicked them off as his hands continued to explore her flesh.

Brody knew that never again would he find this. Sarina was more than just his mate. She'd started out as a passing flirtation and somewhere along the way in the timespan of the blinking of an eye, she'd totally flipped his world upside down. Stunned by her beauty and saturated by love for her, Brody kissed his way from her ankles all the way to her full mouth. Savoring the way her flavor poured through him, Brody ran his warm, wet tongue over her bottom lip, loving the way she invited him deeper with the quick flick of her own tongue. Taking the opening, Brody let his hand slide down her middle as his tongue explored her, tangling with her in a rush to arouse. Her legs parted willingly for him and Brody sank into the heat her body created.

"God you're wet, Sarina," Brody groaned. His fingers dove into her, spreading her wet folds and enjoying the way she panted at his touch. "Give me more, darling."

Brody took her higher, nibbling her everywhere until she writhed beneath his touch, as eager to come as he was to watch her explode. Moving between her legs, Brody used his cool tongue to tease Sarina until she was begging him for it. Sliding his tongue into her while his thumb rhythmically circled her clit, Brody undid everything she knew before. There was so much he wanted to show her. So much he wanted to experience with her, especially the first time she tasted and touched him.

Relentless in his pursuit of her pleasure, Brody continued to taste and touch her, driving her higher as her body yearned and stretched toward completion. Her breathless cries of ecstasy weren't enough to deter Brody from his mission and just as his tongue slid slowly over her small nub, Sarina exploded. Her hips bucked wildly as his name tore from her lips.

"Again," Brody said, sliding his fingers into her swollen folds. He pulled his boxers off and mounted her, filling her instantly, his own need no longer willing to wait. The wet heat of her hot pussy made Brody crave every inch of her and he pressed deeper and deeper still, until she cried his name. Even then he took her again, filling her over and over again.

Brody had never known sex like this. The women he'd had before paled in comparison to Sarina and

Brody felt himself swamped with love for her. The more he filled her, the more he wanted of her. Over and over again he used his hands and cock to arouse her, driving her hard and fast until she shattered around him, her body convulsing around him and drawing his own orgasm from him as they crashed down together.

"I can't… do… anymore," Sarina breathed, her body sweetly wrecked by him.

Brody covered their naked bodies with a sheet and pulled her close, "Just rest with me then." He pressed a kiss to her hair and stroked her arm as they found contentment in the silence. Wondering if she'd fallen asleep, Brody grinned. "I love you, Sarina."

"I love that you love me," she smiled back, pressing a kiss to his side. They slept for an hour or so before meandering downstairs.

"Do you think your family will ever accept you and me being together?"

"It doesn't matter if they do or not. I'm with you, no matter what."

After a quick brunch, Brody took Sarina outside where most of her family was playing volleyball.

"Want to join sis?" Jason asked.

"I don't think I'm quite up for a volleyball game just yet Jay," she smiled. "But give me a couple days and I'll whoop your ass again."

"Too much nookie going on upstairs?"

"Leave your sister alone, Jason Jeremiah," Amanda said, looking at her daughter. "Come sit with me."

Brody watched Sarina sit next to her mother and realized then, how much they looked alike. If it was true that a woman would turn out to look like her mother, Brody considered himself a lucky man. Amanda Traverse, for a woman who was nearly fifty, looked amazing. Sarina strongly favored her, with hints of her father thrown in for good measure.

"How about it, Duscene? You want to play?"

Brody looked at Sarina's twin and noticed some similarities. "Sure," he said, catching the ball as he took his spot on the sand court.

Chapter Six

"He's a good man," Amanda said, nodding at Brody.

"Yes he is," said Sarina, smiling as she watched him.

"Love looks good on you, sweetheart."

"It feels good on me, Mama."

"I don't doubt it, but come tomorrow night you might think differently. Your first season will be your hardest. Being in heat is uncomfortable, to put it mildly. It can often feel as if your flesh will melt off your bones. Brody can help you, if you let him."

"How?"

"The only relief I've ever been able to find," Amanda said with a grin, "is sex."

"You and Dad had sex while you were in heat?"

"You do know why they call it that, right?" Amanda asked, wondering if she'd shared too little with her daughter.

"Because it's the time when I'm most fertile."

"Yes," Amanda smiled, breathing a sigh of relief. "Your body will go through some drastic changes starting tomorrow and lasting about seven days. You'll have moments when it just attacks you and the only relief you'll find is in your husband's embrace."

"But we haven't been married yet," Sarina scowled. "Does that matter?"

"Not when you're mated. You chose him the moment you bit him during intercourse. His bite signified that he in return chose you. The human ceremony is nice, but it doesn't mean anything when discussing the way of the werewolf."

"When was the last time you changed?"

"It's been years. I often stay in my human form for the sake of using my Radiant powers of the Earth. Just as Aunt Penelope, Aunt Briana and Aunt Lucia do. As a wolf, I'm unable to call those powers and with your father around to protect me, I often feel it a better balance to be the witch."

"Will I have powers like yours?"

"You may, although I think they would have manifested themselves before now if you had them. Either way, you're blessed. The wolf is nothing to snivel at. You will make a remarkable werewolf, Sarina. Your father, Brody and I will all be here to help you. Not to mention, you have Jason and all your aunts and uncles and cousins before you who have been where you're about to be. Tonight you should rest, and that doesn't mean sleeping with Brody."

"I can't sleep with him?"

"Not if you're going to love each other intimately. Your body will need the rest for tomorrow night and the days coming after. Without adequate rest, you'll be at a disadvantage to survive your first going into season."

"Alright," Sarina said, sipping the tea her mother had made. "This is wonderful."

"It's a new concoction I've been working on. A mixture of Chi and Jasmine, something to soothe away the aches, whether they be physical or emotional. May I ask a personal question?"

"Sure, Mama."

"Was your first time good for you?"

"I don't know if I'd say *good* necessarily. We were a bit impatient. I do know that in that moment I knew without a doubt that I wanted Brody for my mate. I wanted to know that this incredible man whom I recognized, as if our souls already knew each other, would be mine from then on out. Brody was surprisingly alright with that setup and we mated. I get that Dad thought it reckless, but I couldn't let him go without knowing I'd see him again and soon."

"Your father was an arrogant bastard the first time I met him, telling me I'd belonged to him, not even ten minutes after meeting him."

"Really?" Sarina laughed. "He seems so collected now."

"Thanks to my careful hand," Amanda grinned, giving her daughter a sideways glance before laughing. "He's just matured a lot, is all. Twenty-four years will do that to a person, most of the time."

Sarina wondered how Brody would be in another twenty-four years. Would he settle down well to the idea of a forever mate and the children they made together? The idea of children brought a smile to Sarina's lips. She wasn't jumping at the bit to be a mother, but she couldn't help being fascinated by the prospect of becoming one.

"What's it like to have a baby?" Sarina suddenly asked her mother.

"Shocking," Amanda chuckled. "You and Jason grew so quickly, always fighting for space in my womb. I scarcely knew I was pregnant before you were making your arrival."

"Was it a difficult thing?"

"Scary, as all new things often are. I went into labor so quickly that making it to the hospital was impossible. It turned into the biggest blessing, having you at home. I never imagined myself as a particularly strong person. Even after learning of my powers I just wasn't confident. Then I had you and Jason at home and found an inner strength inside of me that couldn't be put out. After that, I knew I could do anything I wanted as long as I concentrated on putting that first."

"Thanks for the talk, Mama," Sarina said, squeezing her mother's hand as they watched their family play volleyball. "I love you."

"I love you, Sarina."

<<◇>>

The full moon rose slowly, taking its sweet time. Brody and Sarina stood outside her parents' home, hand in hand. He turned to her and said, "I love you, Sarina. I'll be right here the whole time, okay?"

"Okay," she said.

Brody smiled and kissed her forehead as he began to change. In mere minutes he was the wolf that hid inside the man except on the full moon. Howling, he called to the wolves that started to stalk out of the Traverse house. Sarina felt the change in her bones first, a sensation of burning that nearly took her breath away. Then she cried out as her bones began to break and lengthen. Falling to her knees she watched her hands become massive paws and dark blonde hair sprouted all over her body, rendering her clothes useless. The bones in her jaw cracked as her muzzle lengthened to bare the razor sharp teeth of the wolf. Breathless now, she felt the sting of change in her eyes as they switched from the handy eyes of a human to the ultra-keen eyes of the wolf.

When the change was finished, she tested out her new legs, prancing around in circles. Then she bumped into Brody and turned those pretty gold eyes on him. When he nodded to her family, she nodded back and walked stately over to her parents, whom she easily recognized as the alpha and queen. Her father, easily the largest wolf in their pack had a gray tinge to his coat that shone like polished silver. Her mother's dun brown coat shimmered in the moonlight.

Sarina bowed her head before them, submitting both herself and her wolf to their reign. Looking up, it dawned on her that her mother had made the change this time, having done it only once before. In thank you to her mother, Sarina splashed her tongue against her mother's cheek and received the same in return, a smile broadening on the face of the woman inside the wolf. Once everyone knew what they were about, Sarina joined Brody and together they hunted the far side of the property and into the woods that lay outside their community. Normally she wouldn't have ventured that far, but with Brody by her side, having scouted the area plenty of times before, she felt confident that tonight would go well.

They walked amicably together, their tails swishing together in flirtation as they sought out the proper prey. Suddenly Brody lifted his nose in the air and alerted her. Sarina followed him and they soon came upon a clearing where a couple seemed to be enjoying each other. Nearby was a deer that was distracted with the bounty of a clump of berries in a bush. Sarina felt her body ache to spring and she clamped down on the urge as Brody began to stalk toward the prey. Following his lead, she took the other side, staying low in the grass as her mate did. When Brody bounded out, landing close to the couple, Sarina realized that he was after the humans. The deer, having been alerted by their actions, darted off into the woods.

The woman screamed, but Sarina jumped in between her and Brody. She shook her head at Brody and he understood. Humans were off limits. Realizing this, a sense of relief washed over his being and he felt the tension ease from his shoulders. They both turned toward the frightened couple and snarled. The couple quickly got up and dashed off towards town.

After the humans were safely away, Sarina lifted her nose in the air. The scent of the deer was still very strong and she headed off into the woods in pursuit. Brody followed closely but quickly passed her. With both on the hunt, the deer was easily located. Sarina watched Brody claw the deer's neck, tearing deep gashes in the skin and muscle. The smell of blood made her stomach clench. Sarina sank her teeth into the deer's hind quarter, feeling the flesh tear away from the bones. The meat was succulent and rich, a satisfying meal all in all. Brody showed Sarina how to stalk and hunt, necessary skill sets for even the stealthiest wolf. She learned how to work as a team that night.

Curling up under a tall pine, they slept as the moon made its descent and the sun began to rise.

"Sarina," Brody said, giving her shoulder a shake. He'd come up next to her, naked and chilled. She fluttered those pretty blues open and gave him a sheepish smile. "We need to get back before we get caught for indecent exposure."

"Alright," Sarina grinned, noting her own nakedness. "Can I at least get dressed first?"

"Yes," Brody chuckled.

Sarina was pulling on her jeans when Brody cussed loudly. She looked up to see Brody grab his shoulder and yell for her to run. Sarina took off with Brody right behind her. She ran as fast and as far as she could, until her lungs began to burn from exhaustion. Panting, she turned and saw Brody fall to the ground far behind her. Sarina ran back to him and noted that both of his shoulders had traces of silver dripping from them. "Brody," she said, her voice small, even to her own ears.

"They won't kill me, Sarina. Remember that, okay? They can't kill me."

Sarina watched Brody pass out at her feet as a sob emanated from her chest. She stood up and turned around just as the butt of a rifle slammed into her face.

Sarina came to in a dark, dank, musty smell that filled her nostrils. "Brody?" she called, her voice hoarse and scratchy.

She tried reaching out with her mind, but her body was too drained to manage it.

"Good morning, sleepyhead," a man said, his voice cool, condescending. "I hope you slept well because

that's probably not going to happen again for a while.
And don't even bother trying to contact lover boy. He's
so doped up that he wouldn't know whether he was
talking to you or the wall. To him, you're one and the
same now."

"Fu—"

"Well now. I like my women a little feisty. It's been
a while for me, you know. Living alone like I do, I'm
not one for the nookie of long term relationships. I'm
not sure though, that you're quite up for what I have in
mind. Seems to me that you're a little inexperienced in
that department. You don't smell like a woman or a
wolf who has been down that particular road too many
times... although there is always a first time for
everything."

"Tell me where he is," Sarina said, keeping her
voice soft, just enough to sound as if she was pleading.
Truth be told, she was on the verge of tears and was
hoping he wouldn't notice.

"He's around," the man chuckled. "Not here of
course, but he's not dead. You must really like the way
he screws."

Sarina closed her eyes, focusing all of her energy on
breathing. She wouldn't be able to reach out to him
again if she didn't keep herself calm. Losing control
now might doom them both and she needed him.

"*Brody?*" she called in her mind.

"I told you not to try to reach him. By now he's so weakened that I'd be surprised if he can do much more than breathe himself."

"What did you do to him?"

"Me?" the man laughed. "Oh honey, you've got the wrong wolf for that. You need to take that shit up with Reggie. He'd be the one who has your man in chains. Now granted, I like seeing a disobedient wolf in chains just like everyone else, but it's not my job to keep him there. My job is to make sure that everyone I see is doing what they're supposed to be doing. You and your lover obviously weren't. Reggie brought you to me and asked if I'd look after you for a while. I agreed and here we are. Just do me a favor… don't put too much stock in Brody. He's a talented wolf to be sure, but he doesn't have much in the way of staying power. Now, me? I've got stamina out the ass."

"You can take your stamina and shove it," Sarina growled. Suddenly a searing pain shot through her chest, tearing a scream from her.

Sarina shot up in bed, a scream echoing in her head, panting. "Sarina?" inquired the small and mousy voice of her sister Shawna.

"I'm okay," she said. "Go back to sleep." Sarina grabbed her robe and tiptoed to the kitchen, warming a glass of milk to help her sleep.

"Hey pumpkin," Romeo said, pulling out a chair. "Can't sleep?"

"No," she grumbled. "Weird dream."

"Wanna talk about it?"

"I just… I can still feel it and I never remember my dreams, but I'm remembering this one as if it actually happened."

"Want me to get your mom?"

"No. It's late. I can talk to her in the morning."

"You're sure?"

"Yeah."

"Alright. Don't stay up too late."

"I'll try not to."

Sarina, try as she might, couldn't get back to sleep so she sketched instead. Art was something that came naturally to her, like breathing. It didn't seem to matter what she picked up, she could do something magical with it. This time around she'd chosen a set of charcoal pencils. Three hours later, when her mother came down to start breakfast, she'd finished a portrait of the man from her dream.

"Your father said you couldn't sleep," Amanda said. Sarina felt a kiss on her head. Looking up, she smiled.

"Nope. Do you mind if I help you with breakfast while we talk? I sort of want to keep this quiet."

"Sure," Amanda smiled.

"So, I had a dream last night and unlike any other I've ever had, I can remember this one in lurid detail."

"And that worries you?"

"No, not so much really. What worries me is I feel as if it happened to me. You didn't get your powers until you turned twenty-four right?"

"Yes, which I'll remind you, you just did."

"Yeah," Sarina sighed. "But Mama, this dream wasn't just odd. It was crystal clear. Dreams are always choppy, jumping from one place to another, taking people in and out at whim. This didn't and I can't shake the feeling that the man in my dream meant something to me. I can feel him."

"Oh?" Amanda asked. Sarina grinned when her mother's dark eyebrow quirked up at her.

"I was in love with him."

"Oh," Amanda replied. Sarina held up the picture she'd drawn and her mother's lips pursed in response.

"He's handsome. What's his name?"

"I called him Brody and I think we were mates."

Amanda turned, a grin on her face. "That anxious to get started are you?"

"I'm serious Mama. Something happened to me in this dream and I can't explain it."

"Honey, dreams are often seen as messages. Maybe this guy is out there somewhere. Maybe he's not, but either way you need to relax and enjoy this time. Finding a mate is wonderful, but you need to know what you want in one. Spend some time focusing on that and it'll all work out, I promise."

Sarina didn't feel much better, even after a chat with her mother. Something odd was happening. It was like living two different lives, where both of them were happening to her at the same time.

Brody felt as if someone had dipped his body in liquid silver. He'd lost count of the number of times he'd been shot. The silver eventually seeped into his system just enough that Reggie had stopped shooting him. Now he just needed to act as if he was still under the effects of the silver. Thankfully his blood had finally filtered the last of it, leaving him weak, but alive.

"You don't get it, do you? It was never about you bro. It was always about her. I should've just ripped her throat out when you brought her here, but I think the new solution will be just as effective. Of course it'll absolutely suck for you. You'll see her and hear her and smell her, even in your sleep. But you won't be able to touch her or speak to her."

"Why would you do that?"

"She's more powerful than any werewolf or witch I've ever seen. She doesn't know it yet, thankfully. But with a Radiant for a mother and an alpha for a father, Sarina Traverse is the one thing Fenris wanted in his bloodline. The problem is that the bloodline split about five hundred years after he became a werewolf."

"Who the hell is Fenris?"

"He's the first werewolf. He was a regular, non-assuming male, until Lilith, the bitch that she is, took an interest in him. She screwed him six ways to Sunday and then infected him. On the next full moon he made the change and became werewolf. Now Lilith, she was a whore if I've ever seen one, but Fenris did his own fair share of hooking up. He had any number of women in his human form and his seed spread like a wildfire. There was always the one line, however. Then, about five hundred years later, Fenris noticed werewolves showing up from other areas. They were obviously infected and created, but they weren't his. They looked nothing like his wolves. Furious, he tracked down the maker of the new line and killed him, but it didn't stop the line and nothing he did could halt the spread of both bloodlines. You belong to his bloodline. Sarina belongs to the other wolf's line."

"Why the hell does that matter?"

"It matters, because she has a witch, a very powerful witch, for a mother. Mixed with the alpha line of her werewolf father, she'll be virtually unstoppable when she comes into her powers. So, I had someone help us out. Fenris wants his line to swarm the other line and choke it out. Sarina and her family will never let that happen. Fenris arranged a black magic spell to remove all memories of you from the Traverse pack. Essentially, Sarina's memories have been taken and destroyed. She and the rest of the pack won't remember you or your time together. Sarina won't remember that you mated. She won't remember anything after you two met. And if you try to contact the pack, they'll see you as an old and frustrated man, not someone worth an ounce of their time."

"Why not tell me all of this before I met her?"

"You," Reggie chuckled, "weren't supposed to fool around in town that day. You had a job to do, an order to fill. Although, you always were a bit of a loose cannon. Did you think I didn't know about how you'd hunt on their territory? You just couldn't resist the little tart, not that I can blame you. She's hot as hell."

"You've ruined us, you know. As long as she's alive, I can never feel for another woman what I feel for her. And I can't have her, not like I once did. So what's in it for me?"

"Not being dead?" Reggie grinned. "Look, I get that it sucks. Maybe you can learn to be satisfied watching her from a distance. She'll enjoy a full life, probably take another mate someday and live her life until she meets some unfortunate end. Learn to be happy with that."

"Go to hell, Reggie."

Brody's blood boiled and his head felt like it was about to explode. But patience would be his friend for the moment. Brody waited for his alpha to leave before he started yanking at the chains. He pulled and pulled, but the bolts wouldn't give an inch. Even knowing it would hurt and knowing it would probably leave him weakened again, Brody felt he had no choice and started the change. His forearms lengthened and grew thicker as his bones began to shift. He bit his tongue to keep from moaning. When the first cuff snapped, he took his paw and ripped the other one off, freeing himself. Completing the change, Brody decided he needed to face the alpha once and for all. If ever there was a time for the challenge, it was now while his rage fueled his strength.

Brody found Reggie screwing one of the newly changed females. Just into her breeding season with her first change, her human body was wrecked by both the change and her first sexual experience, not that Reggie really took that into account.

Growling, he waited for Reggie to turn around before he pinned him to the wall. Reggie swiped at him with a claw, tearing out three deep scars across Brody's face. Brody punched Reggie in the gut and as the alpha doubled over from the pain, Brody launched an upper cut that caught his foe on the chin. Reggie fell back toward the wall. Looking into the man's eyes, Brody saw nothing good and ripped Reggie's throat out before he could shift. Howling, Brody turned toward the young woman and almost as quickly shifted into a man, not bothering to cover himself.

"Get dressed," he ordered and watched her scramble from the bed she'd been on.

Gathering the pack together, Brody showed them Reggie's dead body and took over as alpha of his small pack. "Gather your things together. We're moving to the New Delta."

"But they already have an alpha and there's no way in hell, Romeo will step down for you," said Reggie's second in command.

Brody growled low in his throat, irritated and tired. "I know that," he said. "My plan is to join our packs. I'm tired of living in this shithole. I want homes and real lives for us. If it means kissing a little ass to get it, then that's what I'll do." Brody didn't add that it'd get him closer to Sarina.

Chapter Seven

Sarina heard the commotion outside and stepped out the front door to see what was going on. "What's up?"

"It seems that this man is the alpha of this little pack. He wants to join ours."

"Why?" Sarina asked Jason.

"I don't know, but Dad's talking with him now."

"Hmm," Sarina mumbled. "It doesn't seem like much of a pack. Maybe they need more numbers to survive."

"Possibly," Jason agreed. "You up for a game of racquetball?"

"Not right now. I didn't sleep well last night and haven't really felt myself lately."

"Alright, Sis," Jason smiled. "If that's the excuse you want to go with to keep from getting your ass kicked, I can live with it."

Sarina, who normally would have jumped at the bait, let it go. She was intrigued by this small band of wolves and wanted to know more. She stepped up next to her father and grinned at the alpha of the small pack.

He was older, but not unfavorably so. His hair had started to go gray at the temples, but his eyes, those were what drew her in. There was something so warm and inviting about them and Sarina found herself entranced by them. What was it about them that made them seem so familiar?

"I'm Sarina," she said, sticking her hand out. The man took it as if it were made of gold, pressing a kiss to her knuckles.

"It's nice to meet you, Sarina."

Turning to her father she asked, "Should I get them some refreshments?"

"I think that'd be wonderful dear," Romeo smiled. Sarina walked back toward the house, the whole time feeling the stranger's eyes on her back. Was there something going on that she didn't know about?

"We need drinks and food for the guests, Mama."

"Can you get them? I'm talking with Aunt Penelope."

"She's not having the baby is she?"

"No. Not yet."

"Phew, for a second I was excited that this day might actually be awesome. Come on, Aunt Pen!"

Amanda chuckled as Sarina poured sweet tea into glasses and arranged three dozen cookies on a tray. Hopefully that would be enough to satiate the small pack outside. She carried the large tray out to the porch and placed it down, inviting people to come and help themselves.

"Thank you," a young girl said as she took a bite of a chocolate chip cookie. Another little boy gulped his tea as if he hadn't drunk anything like it before.

"You're welcome," Sarina said, smiling at the children. She turned from the group, who seemed to be enjoying the treats, and found her father again.

The man's attention almost immediately turned to her. "Thank you very much, for feeding my people."

"You're welcome," said Sarina, giving a slight nod to the leader of the small pack.

"It seems," Romeo said, diverting Sarina's attention back to him, "that Fenris, according to this group's former alpha, had a very, very strong bloodline. However, some years ago that bloodline split into two separate lines. His pack is from Fenris' line, ours apparently, is from the second line. This man, and I think he's on the right track, wants to merge our packs and bring the bloodlines back together."

"How do we do that?" inquired Sarina.

"The natural way. The ones of his pack that haven't found a mate yet, will hopefully find their spouses within our pack and vice versa. By doing so, their offspring will combine our two lines and create one solid line for all werewolves. No matter who or where we are, we'll be amongst family, even if it is distant."

"It's not a half bad idea," Sarina agreed. "How many of his people don't have mates?"

"I'm not sure to be honest. He said that his mate died recently and that may be true for more of his pack, but as he's willing to submit to my authority, I'm going to consult your mother, but we're going to put them up for the night. Can you ask your mom to see to the accommodations?"

"Certainly," Sarina smiled, looking at the older man again. She'd felt attraction before, and he was definitely handsome, but that didn't explain the urge she had to tear her clothes off and ask him to mount her. What the hell had gotten into her?

<<<>>>

"Dad needs to put those people out there up for the night," Sarina said as she walked into the kitchen.

"Alright," Amanda said, smiling. "Aunt Penelope said to tell you that your unborn cousin is just as stubborn as the rest of the Traverse family and that he or she will come when they're damned good and ready."

"Of course. Excuses, excuses." Sarina laughed and helped her mother get everything that they'd need. All the while her mind kept running the handsome, older stranger through her thought mill, desperately trying to figure out why he seemed so familiar.

The next morning, Sarina was up earlier than usual, finding it difficult to sleep once her mind was engaged.

She poured herself a fresh cup of coffee and headed out to the front porch. It seemed that most of their guests had fared well through the night and were now up and busy with taking care of their pack.

"Good morning," Sarina heard, turning to see the sexy stranger. He'd propped one leg on the step and was leaning toward her. "Did you sleep well?"

"Not so much," she smiled. "That's what coffee was made for."

"You can never go wrong with coffee," he returned, his own smile setting her system on overdrive. Who knew that turning twenty-four would boot her sex drive from normal to crazy? Sure she'd looked and even touched some, but this man made her want to do so much more than first base.

"Would you care to take a walk with me?"

"Sure," Sarina agreed.

"Thank you for being so kind. I wasn't sure what to think when I decided to bring my pack under your father's leadership. It's not always easy, especially for a new alpha, like me, to submit to someone else."

"My father values peace," Sarina said. "He's worked hard since Lilith's death, especially, to build peace among the other packs. They stay within their designated communities and so do we."

"It'll be difficult for a while, finding everyone proper shelter."

"We take care of our own," Sarina assured him. "Have you had a chance to meet my family?"

"Not all of them, yet. I noticed a man who looked strikingly like you. And your mother is stunning, much like her daughter. Your father seems fair, but strict."

Sarina chuckled. "Well, the man who looks like me would be my twin, Jason. My mother is beautiful and I've been told that I take after her some. My father is the fairest man I know and yes, he's an extreme control freak."

"So much so that he wouldn't allow me to see you?"

"I don't know about that, but it never hurts to ask. As an alpha, it would be a good start to showing my dad that you're serious about joining our pack and giving up your alpha status," Sarina continued. "Can I ask you something that may sound terribly odd?"

"Sure," he said with a careless shrug of his shoulders.

"Do we know each other? I know that sounds weird and crazy, considering we've never met," she rushed on, "but I just can't help feeling that I know you from somewhere."

Brody looked into her beautiful, intelligent eyes and wanted to jump up and down. Reggie thought he'd been so smart, taking away Sarina's memories of Brody. Apparently, love can't be entirely erased, because she remembered him despite having no clear memories.

"We know each other very well, Sarina," Brody answered as a huge smile spread over his face. "Although, if I were to tell you how, your father might just murder me where I stand as it would sound completely insane and implausible." She leaned close enough to him that he could smell her. Nearly groaning, he stepped back.

"I like insane and implausible things. It means that they're more than likely true," she said.

How had he found a woman like her in such a short time? Witch, werewolf or whatever; she was phenomenal. "I need to talk to your parents, probably your whole family, before we go any further."

The talk that Brody wanted to have, however, had to wait. His people needed provisions and he needed to show Romeo that he was serious about joining his pack and integrating his own.

Romeo and Amanda had felt a familial bond with Brody when he first arrived with his pack. They couldn't understand it, but they were silently pleased when they saw that Sarina seemed to share a bond with this stranger. Amanda tried to use her powers to discern the nature of their feelings but felt that something was blocking her visions. She also sensed that Sarina was the key to ridding this unknown blockage and that it would need to run its course.

"We found several houses for sale in and around the New Delta area. We need to know the financial situation of your pack before we proceed," said Romeo

"Reggie was an extravagant spender. While none of us ever truly went hungry, our accommodations were miserable at best. Our cash and asset funds are almost depleted and our food stores are worthless as well," answered Brody.

Brody heard Romeo sigh heavily and went on. "I don't mean for my people to be a burden to you. I just want them to have a life worth living."

"We'll see that your people are taken care of as if you've always been with us," Romeo assured him.

Over the next six months, Brody worked side by side with Romeo to move his people into the homes that Romeo and Amanda had made available. Seven homes and two near-sized mansions had been purchased under the Traverse name and would now house additional families under his considerable protection.

"I don't think it's over," Brody said one afternoon as he and Romeo moved the last family in. On the way home they'd purchased food for the immediate Traverse family.

"You don't think what's over?"

"The war that's coming," Brody said, inhaling before he continued. "Reggie wasn't a bad leader… he was just a weak one. Instead of seeing to the needs of his people so that we were comfortable, he scraped by on our needs to feed his own selfish desires. He was a line of Fenris and the weakest one of them, I'd say. However, he could be vicious when he wanted to be. He shot me with silver bullets and kept Sarina in chains, until she was finally let go, mainly because the wolf watching her felt badly. Reggie was a lap dog for someone much more powerful. I wouldn't be surprised if Fenris himself was leading a pack somewhere out there, waiting and biding his time."

"Sarina was never put into chains," Romeo said, stopping his truck abruptly. "So would you like to explain why you think she was?"

Brody sighed, meeting Romeo's eyes. "Reggie told me, before I killed him that he'd erased Sarina's memories. He'd taken the last months before we met and shoved them so far down in her memory that she has no recollection of me, my people or anything that happened, neither does anyone in your family."

"I take it you weren't one of my favorite people back then?"

"You won't kill me, will you?"

"Not if what you say is true."

"I met Sarina nearly a year ago. I was picking up an order for Reggie when I saw her walking from a store. Truth be told, I'd smelled her first as she was newly in season and I honestly couldn't resist her. When I saw her for the first time I couldn't believe how beautiful she was. We went to dinner and the next afternoon we met in secret. She paid Joshua two hundred dollars to go to town instead of tagging after her," Brody sighed heavily before he continued. "New to the changes in her body, Sarina was persistent and I was nearly powerless to stop her. She got it in her head that she wanted me, in a forever sort of way. We mated that afternoon. You found out and it made you furious, for good reason. That's when Sarina ran away. I found her and took her to my people, but Reggie said he wouldn't have your spawn in his home. Then he had her shot with a silver bullet. She nearly died."

At first, Romeo couldn't believe what he was hearing. But then he remembered his conversation with Amanda regarding the familial feeling with Brody. His story made sense in light of everything that was going on. Sarina, his little girl despite her age, was a mated woman. Why hadn't he seen her mark? If what Brody said was true, she would need him in another two weeks when she came into heat. "So you're telling me that you and my daughter are tied together? You do realize you're nearly twice her age right?"

"Actually I look nothing like what you see when you look at me. I'm only thirty, sir. For me to be myself, however, Sarina, especially, needs to remember me."

Romeo could easily picture a younger looking Brody in his mind. "Alright," Romeo said, deciding that if this man was going to be his son-in-law, he should give him the benefit of the doubt. "So how do we help her remember?"

"I need to do what we should have done in the first place."

"And that is?"

"I need to court her, to show her the love she feels for me," Brody said. "If I can do that, she'll begin to remember the man I am and I should, in all truth, become the Brody I once was in her eyes."

"What if it doesn't work? What if she doesn't fall in love with you?"

"Then I'll have to let her go," he said.

"And this is you asking permission to see my daughter in an intimate and otherwise romantic fashion?"

"Yes, sir."

"I'll need to talk with Amanda, see if there's anything she can do to help you. However, if there's nothing she can do, we'll go from there. I don't see why it would be too much of an issue. Seeing as Sarina's been walking around the house with moon eyes since you showed up, I don't think it'll be too difficult to let you court her."

"Thank you and for what it's worth, I'm sorry about how everything went down before. Maybe if I had acted sooner, Sarina wouldn't have been hurt."

Romeo grinned. "I suppose I never told you about how I met my wife?"

"No, you haven't."

"Her aunt died and she became the heir to her aunt's estate. My father, being her dad's best friend, had made arrangements through our lawyer, to rent a cabin for her. When she arrived, I was there, along with Joseph, Bryce, Elijah, Audri and Aurora. I told her within the first half hour of meeting me that she would be my wife. Talk about dropping the bomb on someone," Romeo chuckled.

"She was furious, but there was a chemistry between us that was as tangible as this truck. It took less than a week for me to seduce her. She'd just turned twenty-four as well, although it'd been slightly longer for her than Sarina, I suppose. Love is a funny and very powerful force. After we'd slept together, I called the lawyer and told him she'd be staying, which sent her into a fit. She berated me about being her own woman and set me straight on the fact that she wanted a man who could stand beside her and not be inhibited in any way by her strength of character. A few days later she and I mated. That's when she came into her full powers as a witch. Seeing her step into that role was amazing and beautiful. Then we got separated by her half-brother, Dean, and her uncle. Penelope, who was given Radiant powers from her mother, much like Amanda, was there to help her. She killed Amanda's uncle, who was Penelope's own father. He'd become obsessed with finding Radiant powers and killing the witch who had them so he could take them for himself. Penelope, aware of Amanda's existence and the fact that they were cousins, stood up to them, and that day sent her own father straight to hell. Dean of course, survived and came looking for Amanda, along with Lilith, who'd disguised herself as a needy whelp. Once the other Radiants managed to help send Dean to his death as well, Lilith showed her true intentions and made it clear that she'd wanted me for herself all along. Unfortunately, Audri lost Remus, a man she truly loved, in the fight against Dean and Lilith. He'd been seduced by black magic and only at the end of his life had he given his to save Audri. After he passed, however, she was able to mature some and settle down with Benjamin."

"That's one hell of a story. If you don't mind my saying so."

"I don't mind," Romeo grinned. "I can't hate you or even dislike you for falling in love with my daughter, Brody. I've gotten to know you over the last few months and I'd be proud to call you my son-in-law. Whatever Sarina saw in you, I hope she remembers, because I don't think she'll find another man, or wolf, who knows her so well. Good luck to you son."

"Thanks," Brody said with a grin.

Chapter Eight

"Sarina!" yelled Romeo from downstairs.

"Yeah?"

"Can you come down here please?"

"Sure, Dad. I'll be right there."

"Thanks, Sunshine."

Sarina put her pen down and brought her journal downstairs with her, her heart pounding when she saw Brody standing with her father. "Yes, Dad? What is it? Mom left supper on the stove. Aunt Penelope is close to delivering so she wanted to head over that way and check on her."

"That's alright, sweetheart," Romeo smiled. "As you know, we've all been impressed with how seamless it's been to add Mr. Duscene's pack to ours, how well he's done stepping down from his alpha position. On the way home he asked for my permission to court you and I gave it, that is, if that's what you want."

Sarina felt her heart kick in her chest as her lungs worked to breathe. "I'd like that very much," Sarina smiled, a blush covering her cheeks.

"Alright," her father said. Sarina nearly dropped the diary from her hands.

"Would you like to go for a walk, Miss Traverse?" Brody asked with a twinkling smile.

"I would," Sarina smiled. "We won't be long, Dad."

"Make it home for supper. From what I smell, your mother outdid herself again. Plus, I have a feeling that Penelope may be in a rush to deliver that baby."

"Oh I almost forgot," Sarina said excitedly. "I do love new babies."

"I don't know a woman alive who doesn't," Brody said, grinning.

Sarina took Brody's arm and walked out of her parents' home.

"Did I tell you that this home used to belong to my Great Aunt Mabel? She caused a huge uproar when she had a hysterectomy. She loved a human man and didn't want the male werewolves sniffing around her when she came into season, not that it stopped them from doing it anyway. When she passed on, she left the home to my mother. That's how she met my father. My grandfather, Jeremiah, had been Amanda's father's best friend and surrogate brother. When her parents were killed, Jeremiah and my father both watched over her from a distance until she turned twenty-four. That's the year my great Aunt Mabel died. Along with the house, she'd also left a plethora of journals that go back ages and ages in our bloodline."

"Your dad told me the story today, although I'd be interested to hear your mother's perspective on it. He said that he was quite overbearing with her when she'd barely even discovered what and who she was."

"Oh he was," Sarina giggled. "I used to joke about my parent's sex life being like a copy of *Cosmopolitan*, although as I've grown older, I've matured some in that area. Sex is something beautiful, especially in the right relationship. I've always thought it should be an expression of love and not a consequence of lust, or at least not just that."

"You have a very practical viewpoint on it," Brody said, sliding his hand down to intertwine their fingers. When her pretty, dark eyes met his, Brody felt the jolt that went through him, the recognition.

"I've learned a few things in nearly twenty-five years."

"I bet."

"Can I show you something?"

"Sure," Brody agreed with a nod of his head. Sarina liked that about him. She liked that he saw her as an equal, a woman whose opinion and perspective mattered. She chose an open area of grass and sat down, waiting for Brody to join her.

"This is a journal that my mother gave me. Apparently my great-great-so on and so forth grandfather used to keep journals and it passed down through the generations. When my mother gave it to me

I wasn't really sure what to put in it, and then one day I picked it up and just started writing. I don't always use it, but I do quite often."

"Okay," Brody smiled.

"Anyway, about a year ago I wrote in here about meeting a man named Brody who turned my world upside down…

April 24, 2015

I turn twenty-four today. It hardly seems possible. Is this really the year my change happens? Mom says that I'll find my mate when the right man comes along. So far, that hasn't happened yet. Maybe this year. It worked for mom and dad, so there's always hope…

April 25, 2015

I met a man today. He asked me to dinner and I had an incredible time after our initial misunderstanding. He's charming and I'm meeting him tomorrow. Hopefully Joshua will take the bribe and give me some peace and privacy.

April 26, 2015

Why doesn't anyone share the lurid details of sex and mating? I could have used them yesterday. Not that I'm complaining, but it would have been nice to know how wonderfully sore I'd feel today. I never knew there'd be so much inside me. I never knew that love could undo me so easily. I told Brody today and hearing him say it back to me warmed all the cold places inside of me. I've found my mate and I'm never letting him go…

"And this is important because?"

"It was less than a year ago, yet I'm out here with you, being courted by you and I can't for the life of me remember that time. I remember my birthday and the days surrounding it, but absolutely nothing about Brody. Now why would I write down intimate things about a man I don't remember? And I find it extremely odd that you show up here with a pack and your name is also Brody."

"There are things I can't tell you, Sarina. Things you have to know within yourself. You're a beautiful woman and a very creative and smart one. I know that eventually you'll figure out the missing pieces but for this particular situation to turn out well, I'm not allowed to help you decipher any of it. If I do, the consequences could be detrimental."

"So you know how I know you and where from and when, but you won't tell me?"

"It's not that I don't want to, sweetheart. It's that I actually can't. If I were to try, it would all fall apart on both of us and I won't risk you like that."

"Alright," Sarina said. Leaning over, she grinned as her lips met his. Her tongue slid easily over his bottom lip, instantly igniting a passion that engulfed them both, nearly singeing them in the process. Sarina felt Brody's hands wrap around her, laying her back on the blanket as his hand slid under her shirt to cup her warm breast.

Stunned and shocked at the unadulterated need that flashed through her like a backdraft, Sarina pulled back and looked into a face she knew, but didn't recognize. "I don't think I can do this, yet."

Brody felt like someone had dipped him in liquid iron and then dumped a bucket of ice cold water on him. His system was fighting to control the hunger and need she'd let loose with a simple kiss and the cold rejection he'd felt when she said, "No."

"Sarina I… I need to get you home, now."

"Alright," she said, her countenance already changing.

"I'm not angry," Brody tried to explain. "Try to understand that for you this is all new. For me, it's different. I can't give you more details than that, but for me wanting you is as natural as breathing. To be rejected stings in a way I wasn't prepared for, I guess."

"I'm not rejecting you," Sarina said, her voice soft, innocent. "I just… I've waited my entire life to meet a man that I'm comfortable to even think about sleeping with. I shouldn't have kissed you. It's my fault entirely."

"Rarely is anything just one person's fault," Brody said, taking her hand and helping her up. He kept holding her hand on their walk home and said his farewell without touching her again. Kissing her back had been a mistake. She was searching for the connection and moving too fast would only confuse her. Not that a very human part of him didn't want to rush her along. Need gnawed at him like a virus, eating away at his control and resolve. The more he tried to ignore her, the more he focused on being resolved, making sure his people were okay, the more his mind betrayed him. He knew damn well when he'd said he'd never take another female to his bed, that she'd be it for him. He hadn't known that having her would be the hardest and most difficult test of his life.

The next morning, Brody stopped by the Traverse home and found Amanda, the woman he'd been looking for, in her garden. "Mrs. Traverse?"

"Yes?"

"I'd like to talk to you for a minute if I may."

"Do you like to weed flower beds?"

"It's not a passion, but I've done so before." Brody smiled and sat on his knees about five feet from her and started pulling out weeds that worked to choke her pretty plants. "I assume Romeo has told you of my interest in your daughter?"

"He has," she grinned.

"I know you're a very special and talented witch. Have you ever heard of someone's memories being erased to the point that they can remember everything about those times and situations except an individual person or place, time, etc.?"

"I've heard of such black magic, yes."

"Have you ever had success undoing them?"

"The point of the magic is usually to harm," Amanda said. "However, I've found that though they start as black magic, this particular situation can often times test the strength of a relationship. Romeo told me what you confided in him. Let me first tell you that anything he shares with me is strictly confidential. Despite Sarina being my daughter and how much I'd love to spare her the hurt of remembering what she's forgotten, what we all did; I want her to face her own struggle here, because I know how much it will mean to her when she does finally remember what she had with you."

"I may have messed that up already," Brody sighed.

"Oh?"

"She kissed me yesterday when we went walking and I went too far. I scared her and I couldn't… didn't exactly apologize."

"It's a struggle for you as well," Amanda cautioned. "Perhaps even more so. While she doesn't yet remember, you do. It'll be up to you to encourage her in the right direction all the while controlling your hunger and need for her."

"Thank you, for not hating me."

"How could I hate a man who loves my daughter so much?"

"I don't know, of course, but I'd be inclined to hate the man who deflowered my daughter and then got her trapped in a false sense of memory."

"Being a mother doesn't make me an uninformed woman. When I was Sarina's age I was so headstrong. I like to think I put Romeo in his place. We've come to some compromises and agreements between us in the last twenty-five years. I wasn't always the precise and easygoing woman you know. When I was younger, I was so full of passion. Thankfully I learned to direct it at my husband and mate, but I know what it's like to be where you and Sarina are. You'll make it through this and more."

"I hope so," Brody sighed.

Sarina spent the day working with her father on some remodeling that needed to be done in Elijah and Penelope's home to accommodate the new baby. Penelope, being an extremely hands-on mother, wanted the baby's room to have a large open space so that she could transform the nursery into a playroom and keep her sweet little Jeremiah Damon with her. "I never knew being a mother was so exhausting. I don't think I've slept since he arrived."

"He was just born last night, sweetheart," Elijah chuckled, "and you slept when he did. You just don't remember because you never sleep that deep."

"No input from the peanut gallery," Penelope grinned. "So, tell your aunt about this new guy."

"He's just a friend," Sarina started, feeling her cheeks grow pink. "Although I think we'd both like to move it to the next level. I just can't shake the odd feeling I get when I'm around him."

"What odd feeling?"

"The first time I saw him I would have sworn I knew him, his face is that familiar to me. But there are things that don't fit. I wrote last year after my birthday that I'd fallen in love with a man named Brody, but I can't remember anything about him now. Then, this guy's name just happens to be Brody. He's much older than I would have expected myself to be overtly attracted to, not that I'm saying he's unattractive. Ugh, I don't know. I'm sending myself mixed signals."

Penelope laughed. "I remember those times well. Elijah and I could barely get within ten feet of each other without sending sparks off. I could stand in the doorway watching him and practically feel him touching me in his mind."

"Aunt Pen!" Sarina laughed.

"It's true," Elijah chuckled. "I wanted her so bad that eventually being around her became physically painful. I decided it was better to stay away from her than cause us both undue hurt. Then your awesome and brainy mother solved all our problems by proclaiming that a Radiant could marry whomever she wanted."

"My mother did that?"

"She sure did. She'd already been mated to your father so Alessandra and Catrona decided they'd let her be a Radiant and keep your father by her side. Then they passed their powers to their daughters, Aunt Lucia and Aunt Briana. When that happened we all chose your mother as our leader. That's when she changed the rule. She knew my heart's desire was to hold my powers well, while living my life with Elijah."

"My mother is awesome," Sarina grinned.

"And what am I? Chopped liver?" her dad chimed in.

"Dad!" she laughed. "You're just awesome in a different way."

"That's it," he joked. "No more seeing Brody."

"Please," Sarina chuckled. "I'm not sure seeing him is such a good idea anyway."

"Why?"

"I think he wants more from me than I'm willing or able to give right now."

"What did he do?" This came from her Uncle Elijah and it made her heart soar to know that at the drop of a hat, any of her family members would gladly eviscerate any man who hurt her.

"I kissed him," Sarina blushed. "Which admittedly could have sent the wrong message. But he went from being this great friend to talk to, to this hard and hungry man. I wasn't quite ready for that quick a change."

"Here's a note of advice, darling. If you don't want a man to think that you're thinking like him, don't initiate physical contact of any kind. Men have a tendency to think that a kiss means he's getting the whole package," said Aunt Penelope.

"I'm not saying I'm not interested in that eventually-"

"And I'm going to pretend as if my daughter isn't having this conversation while I'm within earshot," said Romeo.

"Please, Dad. I've heard from both you and mom about how your courting ritual went. *You'll only be sleeping with one man, and that's me!*" Everyone laughed at Sarina's spot on impersonation of her father.

"Oh God, stop. I can't take anymore," Penelope laughed. "Sorry Rom, but she got you on that one."

"It's true big brother. Your girl here knows too much. And you were pretty overbearing. I'm surprised Amanda didn't just punch you then kick you out and lock the door behind her."

"I'd just have kicked it down," Romeo said, sticking his head through the door and grinning.

"Doesn't that figure," Sarina smiled. "Alright Dad. I'm going to get going. Mom's coming over in a little bit to visit with Aunt Pen and snuggle baby Jeremiah."

"You'll cook dinner, won't you?" asked her dad.

"I'll make sure we feed the horde," Sarina grinned, hugging her family before she started home. On her way, she saw Brody working in the yard of the home he'd been given. It was a modest three bedroom home that had a pretty yard, one he seemed to be hell bent on keeping well. It was something to notice a man she was interested in being all domestic like.

"It's coming along nicely," she called, giving him a wave from the sidewalk.

"Thank you," he smiled. Leaning on the shovel in his hands, he watched her until she became uneasy.

"Listen, if you're not busy tonight, would you like to come to dinner? We need to talk."

"Sure," Brody said adding a wink. "I need to get these trees in before I shower, but I'll be there."

"See you then," Sarina said, not winking back.

Chapter Nine

Brody got all of his trees in and was able to shower, showing up fifteen minutes early. He straightened his tie and hair before he stepped onto the porch to knock. Before he could do so though, the front door swung open.

"Come on in, Brody," Jason said, a smirk on his face. "Sarina tells us that you used to be the alpha of the pack that joined ours at the end of last year?"

"It wasn't a choice I made lightly," Brody said. "As soon as I took over as alpha, I moved my pack here. I have no desire to lead a pack, large or small."

"Why not? You have it in you to lead."

"It's just not my sort of thing. I have other places to put my passions," Brody said, catching a glimpse of Sarina as she worked in the kitchen.

"Speaking of which," Jason grinned. "My sister can squeeze the last drop of passion from anyone. Be careful around her, bro."

"I know what I'm about with her," Brody assured him.

"If you say so," he grinned. "You want to play some poker? Joshua and I've been playing gin rummy, but if we switch to poker, I can snag all his allowance and I'll even give you a cut."

"Percentage?"

"Seventy-thirty?"

"Make it sixty-forty and you've got a deal."

"Deal," Jason chuckled. "Way to swindle me."

"Nah," Brody laughed. "Just good business sense." Brody and Jason worked Joshua over until the youth was virtually penniless. Then Jason gave Brody his share, which he promptly gave back to Joshua.

"Thanks, man."

"No problem," he grinned. "I know when someone's being played and your brother was dogging you, dude."

"How come you talk so weird for someone so old?"

"Old?" Brody feigned offense. "I'm not that old-looking am I?"

"Sort of," Joshua smiled. "Certainly too old for my sister."

Oh, Brody thought, *little brother's come to rescue his sister's virtue. If only the lad knew he is already too late.*

"I'm actually not as old as I look. I'm only thirty. Just ignore the gray hair and you'll believe me."

"Cool," Joshua said, shaking Brody's hand.

The family ate the lasagna Sarina had made, dipping freshly made garlic bread into the leftover sauce. "This is phenomenal, Sis," Shawna smiled.

"Learn how to cook it yourself and someone could praise you for it."

"Nah," Shawna said, shrugging her shoulders. "Cooking is a waste of time. When I find a mate and settle down, he'll be rich as Midas and I'll hire a cook."

"Good luck with that," Joshua said, taking the words right out of Sarina's mouth and earning him a sharp elbow to his ribs.

Sarina picked up the dishes after everyone had eaten and started the dish water.

"Could you use some help?" asked Brody.

"Sure," she said. "Would you mind unloading the dishwasher?"

"Not at all," Brody smiled. "So, you wanted to talk?"

"I'm one for plain speaking. I don't like beating around the bush."

"Okay," Brody grinned, remembering the first time she'd said that to him.

"I don't think we can see each other anymore."

Brody was floored and more than taken aback. "Sarina—"

"I'm sorry, Brody," she rushed on. "I'm just not ready for the level of commitment and status that you are. You need a mature woman and I'm just not there yet."

"You are there, Sarina," Brody said. Sarina couldn't turn away as he continued. "You are there, darling. Don't you get it? I'm the Brody you wrote about in your journal. I'm the man who loves you, the man who chose you as your mate for life." She felt his hands on her arms as he tore her shirt away. "Can't you see the mark where I bit you? I have a matching one where your teeth sank into my flesh. I won't ever have another woman!"

Sarina felt as if she might heave her dinner right there. But as she stood there, staring at him, she felt a massive and overwhelming heat suffuse her body. Looking around her, the world she knew began to split. Huge pieces of her home sheared off, leaving behind only a dark backdrop. The last thing she saw before her whole world went dark was Brody, screaming for her.

<<<>>>

Turning around, Sarina saw three points of light in the distance. Figuring she had no other feasible choice, she headed that way. Drawing closer, Sarina noticed three doors glowing bright white against the dark. Then, all of a sudden there was a woman standing there. Dressed in glowing white much like the doors, she had almost flaming red hair that hung in spiraling curls against her body, spilling over her back and breasts.

"Welcome, Sarina."

"Where am I?"

"You're in the in-between," the woman said, her lips remaining motionless. "You have an enormous and conclusive choice to make. You'll have the chance to experience each of these doorways for one day and one night. After that period you'll be brought back here to choose the path you'd like to take. The one thing you must remember is that no matter what you choose, there will be sorrowful consequences. You cannot please everyone and should only try to please yourself to a certain extent. Find a harmonious balance between your wants and your needs and know yourself well before you choose."

"What happens when I choose?"

"The choice is permanent as you'll never be given this opportunity again. The next time your world gets torn apart, you'll die."

"I can choose any doorway?"

"Yes," the woman said, her face still expressionless and unmoving.

"I'll take the third door."

"Then open it and step through. You have twenty-four hours to get as much knowledge about this world as possible."

<<◇>>

Sarina stepped through the third door and woke in her bed, a haze over her awareness. Memories flooded her mind as she showered and dressed. Coming downstairs she found Brody, fixing breakfast. "Good morning, Mommy!" Sarina turned and saw her twins, Cadence and Cayden waiting anxiously for pancakes and eggs.

"Good morning, my loves," she gushed, hugging her kids. After snuggling them, Sarina went to the stove and wrapped her arms around Brody's waist. "Good morning."

Brody turned around and smiled down at her. She lifted her face and felt his lips descend on hers. She was just about to sink into the kiss when she heard an audible, "Eww."

"Eww?" she chuckled, kissing Brody again. "What's so *eww* about Mommy and Daddy kissing?"

"It's gross," Cadence said, scrunching up her face in a way that made Sarina laugh. She turned to grab their lunches and grinned when they heard the horn from the school bus.

"Time for learning!"

There was an audible groan from both of her children, but Sarina hustled them off to the bus anyway.

"Come on, before the bus leaves and I have to drive you there."

"And here I thought they'd be gung-ho to head off to school after seeing us kiss," Brody chuckled when she came back in.

"Apparently, us kissing is less offensive than school," Sarina smiled. Hiking herself up on the counter, she gave her husband a come-get-me smile. "Is there any chance you want to do more than just kiss me?"

"Are you kidding me?" Brody grinned, wrapping an arm around Sarina's waist. He pulled her closer, until her legs wrapped around him. He took her mouth with a ripe hunger that poured through him like water to a dehydrated body. Her hips ground down against him and made his jeans unbearably tight as his cock throbbed to fill her.

Her lips parted hungrily for him, inviting him to take what she willingly offered. His hands roamed over her flesh, loosening her clothes so that they slid effortlessly off her body. "Brody," Sarina begged, only fueling his need for her.

Her mouth fused to his, yanking control from his grasp. He wondered for a split second if he'd ever actually had any control where she was concerned. Then the haze filled his mind and nothing mattered in the world except the hot-blooded woman whose inviting body was rhythmically rubbing against him. Grabbing her hips, Brody pulled her down to the floor, her body going molten on him as he continued to touch her. He yanked her suit jacket off and devoured her warm breast through the silky fabric of her dress shirt.

Her moans of pleasure echoed in his ears as he sought to ravage her. Brody felt Sarina's hands on his pants, working the button loose in front so that her hand could slip inside. Then those long fingers curled around his cock and Brody had to fight to take back some control before he spent himself in her hand.

She rose up over him now, a sexy goddess who wanted her own pleasure as much as she'd pleasure him. Running his hands from her hips to her breasts, Brody's eyes nearly crossed in pleasure as she slid hot, wet and ripe over him. Even after two children he still found her wonderfully tight, her pussy able to clench around him in a way that made him grateful he'd been her only lover. Sarina moved up and down on him as he thrust into her, grabbing her hips. She lifted her shirt over her head, giving him a nice view of her beautiful breasts, encased in a lilac colored bra that had matched her panties and the silk shirt she'd had on.

Brody watched her reach up and knead her own breasts as his hands touched her. She brought her body down over him, her mouth tasting the need on his lips. He let his tongue slide past her lips to tangle with hers, fueling the rocking motion of their hips. She covered him fully, almost as if she ached to take him in fully with each thrust. His tongue slid hot and wet over her flesh, encircling the hard tip of her nipples, giving equal attention to both as his hands slid up her back to tug her long, blonde hair.

"Brody!" Sarina breathed as her orgasm bubbled over. She came around his cock and effortlessly pulled Brody with her. He spent himself easily inside her warm depths and smiling, took her weight over his chest. They lay there like that for a few moments before she sat up again, her eyes shining. "I love you, Brody Duscene."

"And I love you, Mrs. Sarina Alessandra Traverse-Duscene."

"You could have just said Sarina Duscene, you know."

"Yeah, but the long version made you laugh and that is one of my favorite sounds."

God, she loved him. To her knowledge she'd never loved anyone before and would never love anyone after him in the same way. She thought of her two beautiful children and knew that her love for them was just as fierce. It was different, but not unequal. The day passed into night and Sarina spent time reading to her children after their baths. She snuggled their tiny bodies, all wrapped up in pajamas and slippers to ward off the cold on the hardwood floors. Then she tucked them into bed, kissing the tops of their heads and whispering, "I love you," to each of them.

"Are they asleep?" Brody asked when she came back down.

"Almost," she grinned. "Our little munchkins have quite active imaginations."

"They get it from you," he smiled.

"Oh no, they don't. I'm as solid as a redwood."

"Uh-huh," Brody grinned. She let him draw her into his embrace, giggling when his lips found the supple flesh of her neck and collarbone. "Make love to me, Sarina. This morning wasn't nearly enough."

Sarina enjoyed an incredible night of love and fell asleep in the arms of the only man who'd ever made her blood burn with desire.

When she woke it was the void of blackness again and she faced two white doors and one red one. "The red door signifies a reality you've already experienced," came the voice of the woman in the glowing white robe. "You may choose your next experience."

Sarina inhaled deeply and looked at the red door for a while before she chose door number one. She opened the door and once again fell into the haze, waking up in bed. After a shower and dressing, she headed downstairs. In the fireplace, the oak logs roared to life, heating the living room and adding charm and romance to the atmosphere. "Are the girls in bed?" came a voice Sarina recognized easily.

"Yes," she said, coming around the sofa. The memories that flooded her mind this time weren't like before. And when she looked at the man sitting in the chair, it wasn't Brody she saw. The shock to her system was one she absorbed, but not without a little trouble. "What are you reading?"

"Nothing important," the man said, standing and approaching her. His lips descended on hers and his hands slid up her back. After that first instant shock, she pulled back.

"Is something wrong?"

"I just… I'm just worn out."

"It's all those hours you've been working," the man said bitterly. "It's a wonder the kids or I ever see you."

Sarina sighed. This was definitely not the reality she wanted. A man she didn't know, didn't recognize. A life consumed by work and a loveless, passionless marriage. She retired early and slept away the night, waking once again in the empty nothingness where two doors now stood red.

"Not every reality is as we wish it to be," the woman said. "We can make it out to be more or less than it is, but rarely can we make it what we wish. There is one door left."

Sarina fell into the reality of the last door and found herself to be an old woman, aged long and hard by an empty existence. Coming downstairs she heard a knock at her door and found her twin, Jason, on the other side. "Morning. Coffee?"

"Yes, please."

"So, tell me what your plans are today? I heard Andrea and Rebekah mention going to the flea market out in Middlebury. You planning on joining them?"

"Probably," Sarina grinned. "It'd be nice to get out and about."

"I should tell you that I saw Brody in town yesterday."

"How is he?" Sarina asked, unable to keep her emotions from swimming into her eyes.

"He seemed well, although I knew he watched for you. I never understood why you two didn't make permanent the love you shared. What happened to you?"

"I was afraid of what was in my heart. Instead of grabbing a hold of it and holding on with both hands for the crazy ride, I let it go for the safety and security that being alone provided. I didn't learn until it was too late that I'd given up a life, for an existence. They are not nearly the same thing."

Sarina spent the afternoon with her sister, Shawna, and her sisters-in-law, wading through the piles of gadgets and gizmos at the flea market. Then she returned home to her empty house, ate dinner, and slept away the night.

<<◇>>

Sarina was back at the place of nothingness. The three red doors were gone and in its place stood a single door that radiated bright yellow sunshine.

"This final door will take you to the reality you most want," the glowing woman said. "Your heart and mind must choose the path you most want to live. Choose wisely as your choice is permanent."

Sarina stepped through the door and woke in her own bed, her memories were those of a young woman who was loved and accepted by her family for who she was. "I think," Sarina heard from her doorway, "that it's time for sleeping beauty to get up."

"I didn't sleep well at all last night," Sarina complained.

"Regardless," Amanda smiled. "You have things to do today. I believe, if I remember correctly, that you have a very important date this afternoon, don't you?"

Her memories intact, Sarina remembered that Brody had asked her out on a date and she'd agreed. "Yes!" she grinned. "What time is it?"

"You've got time to primp, but just. Get ready and I'll make sure you have a lunch packed and ready to go."

"Thank you, Mama." Sarina kissed her mother's cheek and bolted for the bathroom, cranking the shower while she stripped.

"Sarina, Brody's here!" she heard her father call up to her.

"Be right down!" she called back.

Sarina stepped off the last stair and finally saw the Brody she remembered. The man who'd stolen her heart in record time. He stepped up to her and smiled. "You look incredible." His lips found hers and Sarina lost all thought. Pulling back she smiled.

"Thank you," she replied. "You look pretty incredible yourself and I have something amazing to tell you. I need to tell everyone in fact."

Chapter Ten

"Alright," he grinned. She kept her hand in his as her family gathered close. "So, I have no idea what you all remember, but things have been pretty damn weird around here lately. Brody was a man I didn't recognize, Aunt Penelope was having a baby, which is awesome, and I floated into a void of nothingness where a glowing lady made me visit three different realities. One was incredible, one was terrible and the last one was just really freaking lonely."

"What happened?" Shawna asked, always the inquisitive one. Sarina smiled at her.

"I chose the one I wanted most and here we all are," Sarina grinned, leaning over to kiss Brody's cheek. "Apparently setting everything right took some supernatural workings because the woman I encountered was unlike any other I've ever known. She was stunning and it was like looking into the most pure light I've ever known."

"That doesn't sound terrible," said Shawna.

"It wasn't that. It was seeing a world where I was stuck in a loveless marriage or a reality where I chose to be alone rather than risk my heart."

"What about the reality you liked?" Jason asked, curious.

"That," Sarina grinned, "is the lovely thing about this reality. I know where I hope to go and who I want with me when I do. Come hell or high water, I'm going to make the best of this life and love everyone in my life the way I hope to be loved."

"You are loved," Romeo and Amanda said in unison, sharing a smile.

"I know," Sarina gave them all a wobbly smile.

After everyone had gone their own ways, Sarina accompanied Brody on a picnic and told him the finer details of the reality she'd chosen.

"We had twins?"

"Honestly," Sarina chuckled. "I'm surprised we only had two children considering how hot the sex was. I'm glad I can remember it."

"Want to refresh my memory?"

"Absolutely," Sarina laughed, pressing her warm lips to his.

"Wait," Brody said, chuckling when she pouted. "I'm not stopping, just delaying for a second so I don't forget." Sarina watched him inhale and saw a change in his eyes that melted her heart. She loved how easily he shared his feelings with her. All she had to do was look into his eyes.

"It has been one hell of a life since I asked you to dinner. When we mated, I thought it'd be easy to watch you walk down the aisle. Then all this craziness happened and I thought for a long time that I had lost you. I can't tell you the terror that caused in me. I don't want to spend another minute wondering what it'd be like to not live the life I imagine us having. I want to have all of your future, if you'll have me. Will you marry me, Sarina?"

She sobbed through her acceptance speech and when her tears were finally dried by laughter and giggles of joy, she made love to Brody with all the enthusiasm and caring of their first time.

Pounding his fist on the table, the man cursed the Traverse family. Who the hell died and made them rulers of the werewolves and their world? How long had he been trying to destroy them? How many had he sent through the generations to stop their progress? He couldn't come right out and tell them off, smite them where they stood, but if you wanted a job done right and all, you could rarely leave it to someone else. Even Lilith hadn't managed to escape them.

"Get me Dankar," the man said to his assistant who went out without making a sound.

"You called for me, sir," the small, hunchbacked man said, looking at his master at an angle.

"You've studied the black arts for years now and yet these *people* still plague my kind."

"Yes, sire. I have found no permanent solution in the black magic that can destroy that family line completely. The only way to do it is to end the lives of the male children forever. Even then the females will pass those genes on to their heirs as well."

"And yet I have been unsuccessful at every turn in destroying any of them, let alone the whole lot."

"Then perhaps, sire, a more grandiose plan is needed."

"Such as?"

"All-out war?"

"Annoying," the man grumbled.

"Regardless sir, it's virtually unavoidable at this point. You've been trying to take out this line for decades, nay, centuries now. It's time to stop the namby-pamby bullshit and hit them so hard, they never get back up."

"Alright," the man sighed. "Gather everyone so I can address them all and form a plan of action."

"Yes, sire."

Dankar did as he was told and sent word to the fifteen colonies of his master's pack. It took nearly two weeks for them to all gather into the Delta area. He liked being close to his prey, not too close, but close nonetheless.

"They're all here, your highness."

"Thank you, Dankar. Go ahead and keep studying. We will surely need your skills when the full moon comes."

"Welcome!" the man said, his voice booming over the crowd of more than fifteen thousand. It was Dankar's expertise that he never needed a microphone or loudspeaker. "We're gathered here tonight to discuss the annihilation of the Traverse pack. The pack that has plagued our kind since nearly the beginning. Despite my best efforts, I have been unable to find a solution to this problem and have called you all together for an all-out assault on them. I want stealthy intelligence first though."

A handsome young man stepped forward and grinned, his dimples shining. His pretty blue eyes gave off an air of trustworthiness the man was sure would serve him well, regardless of his true intentions. He had jet black hair and when he smiled, the man was forced to admit that he was a handsome devil. "Have you ever thought about infiltration, sir?"

"What do you mean?"

"Their women are beautiful, but hardly are they the strong and more seasoned of our kind. Their oldest female has just become of breeding age. Have Dankar work a spell on her and I promise you sir, I can do the rest. I'll have her wrapped around my finger in days. She'll let me take her to my bed. If I can produce offspring with her, she'll have no choice but to give into your demands, for the sake of her unborn baby, of course."

The man mulled over the young man's idea and grinned. Infiltration would certainly be easier with one of the Traverse women. "Alright," he agreed. "Go and meet with Dankar. You've got exactly two weeks to impregnate the Traverse daughter and gain as much intel as you can about their pack, the numbers, knowledge, so on and so forth."

<<<>>>

Sarina felt as if someone had dropped all of her dreams in her lap all at once. Her Aunt Penelope announced that week that she and Elijah were expecting a beautiful baby boy and Sarina told them his name before they ever said anything, a smile of knowing on her face. She had fixed things with Brody and her body felt sanguine as she stripped for the shower.

"May I join you?" came a sultry and very masculine voice. Turning she saw Brody standing there. He looked different today, dark and dangerous in a way that made her body hum with expectation.

"Gladly," she grinned. Turning the hot water on, she cranked on the cold and adjusted the temperature. She stepped beneath the spray as the hot water hit her flesh. She heard the shower door open and felt Brody step behind her. His hands massaged her shoulders and she moaned when his lips touched her flesh. He kissed her from shoulder to shoulder, slowly turning her on as his hands found the perky roundness of her breasts.

He teased her nipples, rubbing her tight peaks between his thumbs and forefingers. Her head fell back against him as her ass bumped against his aching cock.

When he bent her over, Sarina gladly acquiesced, feeling the thick press of his tip against her yearning pussy. The first thrust was hard and deep, filling her in a way that tore a moan from her chest. He pulled out and pressed in again, setting a savage rhythm that made Sarina grab at the walls and faucet for purchase. "Oh baby," Brody groaned, filling her over and over again. He slammed into her, his shaft taking her in a way they'd never touched before and Sarina felt her body boil over as her orgasm screamed through her body.

"Can I steal Brody for a minute?" Sarina smiled, addressing her father.

"Sure, honey."

"Are you okay?" Brody asked.

"I'm wonderful," Sarina said, wrapping her arms around Brody's waist as they walked. "I just thought that telling you you're going to be a father might be something you'd like to hear."

"What did you say?" he asked, stopping and facing her.

"We're having a baby," Sarina said, "I'm nearly eight weeks pregnant!"

"We're having… a baby," he whispered almost reverently.

"Isn't it wonderful?"

"Your dream thingy," Brody said. "Is it twins?"

"I don't know, yet."

"When can we find out?"

"In about three days, when I go see Aunt Briana."

"I'm going with you," Brody said, his face leaving no qualms about what he wanted. "Wherever you have to go, I'm going with you."

"I wouldn't have it any other way."

Brody kissed her soundly, pressing her up against the building at her back and plundering her sweet mouth.

"I think," Amanda said as she and Romeo dressed for bed, "that very shortly here, our oldest is going to announce an upcoming arrival."

"Please not yet," Romeo nearly winced.

"We're ripe for grandchildren," Amanda grinned. "Can you imagine little ones running around here again?"

"Shouldn't we get our oldest out the door first?"

"You know darn well you and Brody have been working like dogs on his home. You can't blame him for wanting the best for her. Would you rather he be a lowlife?"

"No," Romeo sighed. "Letting go isn't nearly as easy as I thought it would be."

"We're not letting go," Amanda assured him, "We're just opening our arms a little wider."

"If you say so," Romeo grinned. "You wanna open your arms wider?"

"Come here, lover boy."

As Amanda and Romeo enjoyed each other, the spy slinked back to his master with information that was badly needed.

"His daughter is pregnant. Now whether it's my seed or her mate's I'm not sure, but either way, she's expecting. Taking any of them out would be a bonus, but catching their youngest breeder would be a coup and you could easily break them then. If I've learned anything about this family, it's that breaking their spirit makes breaking their physical ranks so much easier."

"You've done well," Fenris grinned. "Surely we'll have them taken down in a short time now."

"I can already see the end sir. And may I suggest congratulating Dankar on a job well done? Sarina Traverse never even suspected that I wasn't her Brody. And she puts out like a wolf in heat, even when she's not. I don't mind saying that I'd screw her six ways to Sunday if given another chance."

"I'll congratulate Dankar in due time," Fenris agreed. "For now, you may bed any female in the pack you wish, whether to screw or mate, is up to you."

"How long can I keep her?"

"If you mate with her, forever. If you choose only to take her to your bed, you'll have to accept my good graces for as long as they last."

"Alright," Brandt said. Walking through the halls of the huge mansion Fenris had built an eon ago, he smiled. Remembering how it'd been with Sarina, he felt a need claw its way into his system. He turned the corner and saw a lovely little blonde standing there. "Hello," he smiled. She blushed and curtseyed, her breasts nearly falling out of her top. "Would you like to know a secret?"

"Sure," she smiled.

"Fenris has given me permission to take any female I wish as my mate."

"Oh," she said, her pretty blue eyes going round with surprise. Brandt could already feel the ache to touch her, to take her. "I hope the fortunate woman knows how lucky she is."

"I do as well," he grinned. Holding out his hand to her, he walked with her a ways. "What is your favorite pastime?"

"I like all manner of things. Arts, politics, racquetball. If it interests me, and most things do, I enjoy it."

"Does sex interest you?"

"I'm not of an age to breed yet, sir."

"I didn't say breeding. I asked if sex interested you."

"Yes, sir." Brandt watched the girl blush and need knifed through him.

"Good," he smiled. "What's your name, darling?"

"Sadie, sir."

"Call me, Brandt. Come with me won't you?"

"Yes, sir."

Brandt took her to his room and offered her a glass of wine, which she accepted. "I've never seen the upper class chambers. They're beautiful."

"They are, I suppose. I don't much care for anything in here save the fireplace when it's needed and the bed of course. I find it the most comfortable for showing a woman how it should be. I have a need for you."

She blushed crimson and Brandt took her hand. "I want so much to show you how good it can be between us. Will you let me have you, Sadie?"

"Yes, sir."

"Call me Brandt," he said, his voice sterner.

"Alright, Brandt," she said, stiffening her spine. Taking her mouth, Brandt plundered her roughly as his hands stripped away her clothes. His hands bruised her flesh as he lay her down on the bed. Lying down next to her, he sank his fingers into her center, plunging into her until tears ran from her eyes.

"You're so lovely, Sadie. Open yourself to me." Pulling his hand back, Brandt made love to her gently now, slowly opening her wet core. He buried himself inside her, filling her completely and tasting the salt on her breasts with the tip of his tongue. He took her over and over again until she came hard, squeezing his cock until he exploded.

Not sated, he touched her everywhere, exploring her beautiful body as memories of his time with Sarina played through his mind. He took her over again, explaining how it would be between them if she'd mate with him. "When we join and it builds between us, we must bite each other, therefore marking us as mates."

"Okay," Sadie said breathlessly as his fingers played over her swollen clit. He rode her a little harder this time, needing the roughened, hard edge of her orgasm. On her climax, he sank his teeth into her neck and tasted the hot flavor of her arousal. Only Brandt had lied. He'd said that they'd need to bite each other, but Sadie never got that far as Brandt changed, snapping young Sadie's neck and ending her life.

<<<>>>

Sarina and Brody went to see Briana, the Radiant, the next week and learned that they were indeed having twins.

"It looks like a boy and a girl," Briana smiled. "Congratulations."

"Thank you," they said, smiles on their faces.

"You're welcome," she grinned. "I can imagine your parents are thrilled. I know how much your mother loves children."

"She's over the moon and we haven't even told her about the twins, yet."

"Well. We'll see you rested and home before you know it," Briana smiled.

The next morning, Sarina and Brody headed home, their news spreading joy through the entire family.

"To a new generation," Jason said, holding his champagne in the air.

"To the future," Romeo added and everyone, save Sarina, enjoyed the bubbly.

Little did the Traverse family know that somewhere in the darkness, a force was planning to end the future they were celebrating and Fenris, a wolf they'd thought to be long-dead, was leading the cause.

-*To be continued in Book 2*-

If you enjoyed this title, I would appreciate your leaving a review of the book. Good reviews encourage an author to write as well as help books to sell. Good reviews can be just a few short sentences describing what you liked about the book without having a spoiler. If you could spend 30 seconds writing a review, I would appreciate it: you can review this title right now at your favorite retailer.

Here is a preview of the **next story** you may enjoy:

Alpha Infiltration: Romeo Alpha Blood Lines Romance, Book 2

"**YOU LOOK** awfully chipper this morning," Jason Traverse said to his twin when she strolled through the front door.

"Why shouldn't I be?" Sarina asked. She quirked an eyebrow at him as if to emphasize her point.

"Being pregnant, I'd think you'd be miserable," Jason smirked. "At least I sort of hoped you would be."

"Jerk," she said, teasing. Rounding the corner, Sarina greeted her mother, who was already up preparing breakfast.

"All grown up and still the bickering never stops," Amanda Walker-Traverse said, grinning at her daughter. "You do look lovely Sarina."

"At least someone in the family knows beauty when they see it."

"You get it from me, so it's only natural that I would," her mom said, laughing. "How's Brody?"

"Running around like a mad wolf. He seems to think these two will grow fast like Jason and I did."

"Well, werewolves do tend to grow much faster than their human counterparts," Amanda said, giving Sarina a gentle reminder.

"I know," she agreed. "I just don't think we need to baby proof the house today, or have a nursery ready yesterday. Brody insists on it so I just stay out of his way."

"I'm happy to know that he cares so much for you," Amanda said with a smile. "I have to admit there was a time, not so long ago, that we all worried that you'd made a mistake. Then, when you went through that period of forgetting when none of us knew who Brody was, it was just odd. Now that everything's back to normal, I can take a step back and tell you that you chose wisely. It was brash to say the least, but you knew your mate and never faltered from that decision."

"Thanks, Mama. Now if only Jason here could find himself a mate."

"Who says I haven't?" Jason said defensively. "I have a woman in mind. It just so happens not all of us are ready to jump on the matrimonial bandwagon as of yet."

"Oh please," Sarina scoffed. "I'll take my dying breath before you ever take a mate. You'd much rather just take a woman to your bed without all the trappings of a relationship. I know."

"I'm not denying that having a woman in my bed is nice, but lately I've come to realize that there's more to life than a couple of hours of passion in the night."

"Welcome to reality little brother," Sarina smiled.

"Can you two please talk about something other than sex at eight in the morning?" Amanda said.

Sarina took a seat close to her brother and thanked her mother for the French toast she'd been served. "This is amazing."

"You always say that," Amanda chuckled.

"That's because I'm always right," Sarina winked. "These two want more." She gestured to her belly.

"I was ravenous when I was carrying you two," Amanda said. Sarina watched her mother with a smile on her face. She'd taken her mother for granted, that much she knew. Still stunning at almost fifty in human years, Amanda was a picture of beauty. The way she moved showed strength and grace. Her hair still lustrous and dark as mahogany. Her eyes still sparkled when she smiled, which she did often, especially if the children's father was close by. "I'm surprised your father didn't kick me out when I got pregnant with Wade."

"Please," Sarina laughed. "Daddy's been crazy about you since day one. I've never seen any signs of that changing. If I didn't know better, I'd say you two are still on your honeymoon."

"We are darling," Amanda laughed. "Well, maybe not, but we're still over the moon about each other and we both know it. When you choose a mate there is no other who can turn your head."

"You're getting awfully sentimental on us in your old age, Mother," Jason teased. One look from her had him clearing his throat and stuffing his mouth with French toast.

"Careful now, pup," Romeo said with a grin as he entered the kitchen. "Old age or not, I'd still lay money on your mother to give you a good ass whoopin'."

"Yeah, yeah," Jason said with a wary smile.

Sarina loved these moments. It was one of the many things she'd miss now that she and Brody had finally finished moving everything into the home he'd been given when he'd conceded his leader status. Brody, Sarina's mate, had killed Reggie, the former alpha of his pack and taken over, all with the sensible intentions of bringing his pack under the tutelage and ruling right of Romeo and Amanda. As King and Queen of the Delta packs, it was only right that his pack join them. Since doing so, his pack had wanted for little and seemed even more settled than he'd ever seen them. Instead of living in caves like dogs, he was happy to report to Sarina and everyone else that his former pack was elated with how things turned out. They'd been given homes, food, necessities of everyday life and overall, they'd been well taken care of.

Brody, in exchange for his submission, had been given prominent status within the pack as a general. He helped Romeo keep the pack together and content, working as a liaison for those who lived further away from New Delta, making sure everyone had the necessities they needed. For her part, Sarina was happy to be pampered as her unborn twins continued to grow strong and rather quickly. She wasn't sure they were developing as fast as she and Jason had, but she was already showing and they'd only found out about the babies a month ago. At the rate she was going, it'd be well under half of the normal human pregnancy term when she would be ready to deliver. No wonder werewolves multiplied so quickly.

Finding her mother after breakfast, Sarina voiced her concerns. "I'm thinking about asking Brody if we should stay near the hospital from April on until the babies arrive."

"That's not a bad idea, although having them at home isn't a bad option either. I learned a lot about myself when I was having you. I found a confidence and reliance on myself and the ones I love. I probably wouldn't have noticed had I not been able to deliver you as I did."

"It's scary this first time."

"It's always a little bit of an anxious time, although I will say the first time there is always the unknown. I will support you in whatever you decide, Sarina."

"I'll see what Brody says and let you know from there."

"You do that, sweetheart. Meanwhile, I've got some major craft projects to get started if we're going to have these babies taken care of when the time comes. Never let anyone tell you twins don't run in families."

Fenris sat back and contemplated his next move. Sending the young buck, Brandt, to seduce and impregnate Romeo's eldest had been a stroke of genius on his part. Now to wait and see if the seed she carried belong to Brandt or her worthless wolf of a mate. Fenris was already smiling, just thinking about it. It wouldn't truly matter of course. He'd rip them apart no matter whose seed she carried.

He'd thought long and hard over the last several weeks about how to go about his first strike. He wanted it to hurt… a lot. Romeo needed to know and understand that he was not the alpha in charge. It wouldn't be easy, as taking down any alpha never was, but Fenris knew that given the alternative, Romeo would bow his knee to him.

He could almost see that moment and could admit that it turned him on. Having the play of any female he wished, including Romeo's sweet wife, or even one of his succulent daughters. Brandt had howled for days about the one called Sarina and how beautiful she was. Fenris couldn't blame him for getting hooked on her. An alpha's daughter was no small prize and if she was beautiful and put out as hotly as Brandt proclaimed, Fenris himself might even give her some enviable attention.

At any rate, Fenris knew that his first strike had to be the hardest and most elusive. If he did it right, and he damn well would, Romeo Traverse and his family would have no choice but to submit to his ruling. The thought of ruling the entire Delta area sent a ripple of fire through his blood as he thought about making the Traverse family pay. They'd been a thorn in his side ever since they'd split from his line. Now he'd finally worked out a plan that would set things right. He could hardly wait to get started.

"Dankar!" Fenris shouted. His patience, he could admit, wore thin during times when he was thinking about what was coming.

"You called for me sir?"

"I need you to do whatever it is you did to Brandt again. It needs to be perfect and if you can manage a longer time, that'd be in your best interest as well."

"I'll get right on it, sir."

"See that you do."

Brandt met Dankar in his quarters. "You wanted to see me, Dankar?"

"Yes, yes," the small man said. "Come, sit."

Brandt did as he was bade and sat in the chair where Dankar had worked on him the last time. "I presume that Fenris wanted you to make me like Brody again?"

"Yes," Dankar replied, his tone short.

"Remember, Dankar, you may be Fenris' right hand man, but it is I who watches your back. Show some damn respect."

"Yes, Brandt," said Danker, but guardedly this time.

Brandt watched the little man mix potions and concoctions of who-knew-what brew. The noxious fumes were almost enough to make him pass out. He hoped that whatever it was that Dankar was doing, that it worked well and fast, because the last thing he wanted was to have to drink some nasty shit.

"This may not feel nice," Dankar said to him as he injected him with a large dose of some neon fluid. "But it should let you have an uninterrupted two weeks with Sarina and her family. Don't screw it up"

Brandt went back to his room and awaited the change he knew was coming. The first time had been less than pleasant as his body shifted into that of the alpha's daughter's mate. He'd had twenty-four hours last time. If he had to account for fourteen days, this was going to royally suck. Like most synthetic drugs it took nearly twenty minutes to feel the effects, but once they started, Brandt could hardly breathe. Even going from man to wolf, his change always started in his eyes.

Pain shot through his irises and into his optic nerves as brown turned to blue and his pupils dilated. With his pupils the size of dimes, he was thankful his room had no windows. The light he had forgotten to shut off streamed into his vision, making Brandt curse as he swiped a hand down the wall, desperately trying to find the switch. "Shit!" he growled as his body, relentless under the pressure of the drug's interference, continued its change. His shoulders widened and his torso and legs lengthened. The muscles in his arms, thighs and abdomen stretched and added new tissue as his body grew from a modest five foot eleven, to the taller

Brody, who easily stood six foot, three inches. His jaw cracked and widened, giving him the strong jawline Brody sported. The hair on his head grew thicker, sprouting thousands of new hairs to add the lush texture of Brody's dark locks.

Two hours after it had all begun, Brandt was finally able to look in the mirror and see Brody standing there. His eyes, now crystal blue, smiled when he did. The facial hair, dark in texture and color, much like his hair, was easy to shave. He knew from watching, that Brody rarely wore a beard or let his facial hair grow much past a five o'clock shadow. He scowled, smiled, frowned and made every facial expression he could think of to make sure the process had changed his physical appearance in every way.

"It looks as if all went well," Dankar said, standing in Brandt's doorway.

"Screw you," Brandt said, glaring at Dankar. "The only solace I have is that I have two weeks to forget the pain. I may want to kill you when I change back. Be mindful to keep your distance from me when I do."

"I won't forget," Dankar said. Brandt could have sworn a grin crossed the man's face. If he didn't know better, he'd lay money on the pain being the most enjoyable part for Dankar when he concocted his potions. He had yet to use one that didn't have some sort of pain with it.

If you enjoyed this sample then look for **Alpha Infiltration: Romeo Alpha Blood Lines Romance, Book 2**.

Here is a preview of **another story** you may also enjoy:

Romeo Alpha: A BBW Paranormal Shifter Romance - Book 1

AMANDA WONDERED how the hell she had gotten so far away from home. When she walked, she usually didn't go past a couple of blocks, but she felt so different today. Something was pushing her further and in a different direction, and she wasn't sure what it was. But she didn't care at the moment, because she just wanted to walk.

Not thinking twice about where she was going, she let her gut instinct give her the direction she needed.

Her grandmother had always told her to go with her gut. She'd said human instinct was better than anything. "Intuition is a girl's best friend," she would say, and then they would both laugh. Talks she and her grandmother had always seemed to pop into her head at the strangest of times, like now.

Here she was, going for a walk, and wondering why she wanted to go in a different direction, and there was her grandmother's voice in her head, propelling her along. Amanda missed her grandmother more with every passing year.

Amanda paused and thought about her life thus far. She had just graduated from college and started working in the local animal hospital, but it wasn't quite like she had thought. She didn't see the care and passion she'd hoped to find in the industry. In the city, being a vet was all about how much money you could make, how many pets you could treat. And, at twenty-four, it was hard to be taken seriously.

Her two female roommates were nice, but they all just went their separate ways. They didn't eat ice cream and watch movies like on *Friends*. They didn't share secrets or even laugh or hang out. They really just slept in the same apartment, and they usually weren't even home at the same time. Except Amanda, that is.

Amanda was always at home, it seemed. She had nowhere else to go, really. The other two girls spent most nights out with their real friends or their boyfriends. Amanda lived a lonely life, but she was happy. At least, she was pretty sure she was happy. After all, she had an upstanding career, and she still had money left over from her savings.

Both her parents had been killed in a car accident years ago. Amanda had graduated from high school with no family there that day or on the day she graduated from college. It was what it was, though, and she knew that her parents watched her from Heaven.

The only positive thing was that her parents had been prepared and had made sure they left enough money and a big enough life insurance policy to help her out. They would be surprised but happy knowing how much that money had helped her in the years after their death. She was proud to say that she was able to live off of it through her college years. She'd never even had to get a job like most kids did. Amanda had been able to focus on her classes.

That freedom wasn't worth it, though. She would have worked three jobs at a time while going to school for one more day with her parents.

However, the account was finally starting to dry up, and she needed to think about what she would do. Sure, she had a new job that could pay her bills, but those loans were piling up with interest. Even a vet job only went so far.

Amanda sighed as she began the trek back toward the house.

Amanda liked her walks in the evening. It helped her to relax, enjoying the quiet time alone. And while Amanda wasn't overweight by any means, it helped slim her waistline, which showed those extra biscuits she liked every now and again.

She turned and began to make her way back to the townhouse she shared with her roommates, but stopped as she heard a noise

A rustling came from behind her, and she turned to see the bushes shaking. Looking over to the other side of the sidewalk, she saw those bushes shake as well. Not wanting to wait around to find out what was behind the leaves, she took off at a run. She swore she heard a growl come from behind her, but she didn't turn to see what was chasing her. That would only slow her down. As she reached the door to her home, she quickly turned the knob and went through headfirst. Shutting the door quickly, she looked out the window. She got a glimpse of a long black furry tail as something ran around to the side of her building.

"What in the world are you doing, Amanda?" Betsy stood there looking at her inquisitively.

"Something was chasing me."

"What?"

"I don't know what it was, but something big and furry was chasing me. I saw a long black tail just now when I walked into the house."

"You mean when you dove into the house?" Betsy's grin faded. "I'll call the game warden. If there is a big animal outside, then none of us need to go out there until they find it and get rid of it."

"Well, I don't want them to kill it."

"I know, silly, but if it's a wild animal, they can take it out to the National Forest and let it loose. The city is no place for a wild animal." Betsy turned and picked up the phone from the receiver.

Amanda stood in shocked silence as she listened to her roommate tell the person on the other end of the phone what had happened.

She knew from Betsy's tone that she and the person on the other end of the phone were questioning her sanity. They lived in a big city, and the closest thing they got to a wild animal was a stray cat or two. They didn't even get raccoons. If there was some huge animal like she thought, then it would make headline news.

Shaking her head in aggravation, Amanda turned toward her room. She suddenly felt silly and didn't want to have to explain what she saw to any more people.

"Amanda? Where are you going? They are on their way and might need to talk to you."

"Tell them it was a dog. Now that I'm thinking about it, it kind of looked like that couple that lives down the road's greyhound. Maybe he just got out."

"Are you sure, Amanda?" Betsy asked, turning and saying something into the phone.

Without saying another word, Amanda shut the door to her room tight and then quickly locked the door. She looked over her room and, seeing the window open and the curtains blowing in the breeze, she ran over to push the window pane down and lock it tight. As she stood there, she looked out into the woods that made up her backyard. There, in the distance, two yellow eyes stared back at her.

Suddenly, more eyes appeared, and it seemed the animals went on forever. She was amazed, since the woods behind her house were very dense and small. The dark night was lit with a full moon. A shiver raced through her as she stood there and stared into the first set of yellow eyes. She quickly shut the curtains and went to sit on her bed. She didn't think she would ever be able to fall asleep knowing what was out there. As she laid her head on the pillow, her mind wondered to large beasts with yellow eyes and sharp fangs. But she was soon fast asleep.

<<◇>>

Amanda awoke with a yawn. It had been almost a month since the incident with what she now called a dog. She had agreed with Betsy that her mind had been playing tricks on her that night. There were often times when she was sure she felt eyes on her, and she would turn in one direction or another, looking. What she was seeking, she didn't know, but somewhere in the back of her mind, she just wanted to know if the eyes she had seen that night had been real or just part of her dreams that evening. She was still so uneasy about it that her walks seemed to get earlier and earlier each evening.

She was just about to walk out the door when her phone started ringing. She quickly grabbed it and pushed the button to answer it.

"Hello."

"Ms. Walker?"

"Yes?"

"Hello, Ms. Walker, my name is Ernest Montgomery. I am calling to tell you that your aunt has passed away."

"My aunt? But I don't have any family. You must have the wrong Ms. Walker."

"No, ma'am. Your father was Joshua Walker, correct? Mother Maureen Walker?"

"Yes."

"Then, I have the right Ms. Walker. It is your father's sister I am referring to. She unexpectedly passed away from a heart attack. I am very sorry for your loss."

"Oh, my gosh! I never knew I even had any family.
I am very sad that I didn't get to meet her."

"Yes, ma'am. I'm sure. She was a nice woman. I
have also called you to see if you can meet with me. I
need to go over her will with you."

"Her will?"

"Yes, ma'am. Your aunt was a wealthy woman."

"Oh? Um, okay. When would you like to meet?"

"The sooner, the better."

"Okay. How about today?"

"That would be great. I am in Slatesville, in the
valley. "

"Oh. Okay. That is just forty-five minutes from me.
I can be there in a couple of hours."

"Sounds good, ma'am. I am at the *Montgomery Law
Firm*. I am the only attorney in the town."

"Okay. Thank you, sir. I will see you soon."

"Yes, ma'am. I'll be waiting."

Amanda fell back on the couch, stunned, for what
seemed like forever. Everything was pushed to the back
of her mind as she thought about what she had just
learned. She had a family. Well, she *did* have a family.
Now her aunt was gone. Could there be others in her
family who she knew nothing about? She didn't know,
but she did know one thing. She wasn't going to find

out sitting around here, twiddling her thumbs. She needed to get going fast.

Amanda headed for the kitchen. She wasn't surprised to see that no one was there. Of course her roommates weren't home. They were either in class or with their boyfriends.

Smiling, she made a cup of coffee and drank it slowly, thinking about what she might find out. Then, with a deep sigh, she made her way to her car. She looked at the small Honda with pride. It was a pile of junk to some, but it held a special place in her heart. She hadn't been able to get rid of her father's car. Instead, she had sold her own.

She looked down at the small picture he had taped to the dash near the speedometer. She was about six in the picture, and she had been holding her mom's cheeks in her hands as she kissed her.

She remembered the day like it was yesterday. They had just got to a cabin they vacationed in. She had enjoyed herself so much. The little cabin had one bedroom with a queen-sized bed where her parents slept and a set of bunk beds for her. They had stayed up late roasting marshmallows as her father told her scary stories about wolves and vampires. She had ended up in their bed, snuggled between the two of them. They had spent the next day hiking and walking trails and seeing tons of waterfalls and animals.

She had loved it and had never forgotten. It soon became a family tradition to go camping every year. After some of those trips, they didn't return home.

Instead, they moved on to a different location. The constant moving had been hard on her as a kid, but she would have never told her parents that. She had felt like they were hiding something from her. Of course, she had been young back then and had blown it off as childhood curiosity. Now, with this new family member, she wasn't so sure.

Her parents had been very quiet people. They seemed cautious of everything going on around them and were even a little jumpy at times. Maybe there was more going on here than she thought. She needed to find out.

She wiped away a tear and go in the car. The car had a huge dent in one side and was almost fifteen years old, but it got her where she needed to go. She slid the car into drive and smiled to herself.

"Dad would be proud that his car was still running so good, wouldn't he, Trixy?" She and her father had named the car together.

Amanda turned onto the next road and made her way down the narrow two-lane road that led into the mountains. She had never been this way because her parents always went the long way around the mountains. They said they liked to take the scenic route.

She came to a small wooden sign that said *Slatesville—Welcome to your home away from home*. She smiled at the welcoming sign and kept on her way to the town. As she drove, she was amazed at how beautiful everything was. The low-hanging branches of the trees scraped the roof of the car every once in a while.

She was amazed at how many animals she saw. Deer acted as if they weren't afraid of her car. Raccoons were plentiful, and she jumped when a large black snake slithered across the road. There were people all around, and they watched her car curiously as she made her way down the street.

The town reminded her of a long lost western ghost town. It was a little spooky, and she caught herself checking the doors to make sure they were locked. The men nodded at her as she moved forward and many of the people smiled, although they held themselves back a little.

Amanda finally saw the sign that said *Montgomery Law Firm*. She pulled into one of the many vacant parking spots and slowly got out of the car. A handsome man leaned against the building she was about to enter. His brown eyes had flecks of yellow and orange in their deep depths. She smiled slightly, and the man just continued to stare as he looked her over slowly.

"Can I help you, ma'am?"

"I am just here to see Mr. Montgomery."

"Well, you're in the right place, Miss…?"

"Oh, Amanda. Amanda Walker. And you are?"

Something changed in his eyes as he smiled at her and made his way to her side. He held out his hand to her. "Name's Curtis Livingston."

"Oh. Do you live here?"

"Yes. I'm one of the controlling partners here in Slatesville. Well, I have to be going. It was good to meet you."

"You, too, Mr. Livingston."

"Please, call me Curt. Everyone does."

"Only if you call me Amanda."

"That's a deal, sweet lady." She flushed all over when he raised her hand to his lips and gently caressed her knuckles with a brief touch of his mouth. She felt the rise in temperature in her cheeks spread across her upper chest. She stood there and watched as he walked away from her down the street to slip inside a store. She felt foolish and realized that she had been staring. She shook her head, trying to think straight and clear the thoughts that were running through her mind.

Amanda was always aware that she wasn't the Barbie doll type of girl. Although she wasn't fat, she wasn't rail thin, which most men liked, either. Her waist and stomach didn't look like a washboard, although it didn't look like a bunch of bread dough either.

She instantly felt inadequate and quickly turned around to walk to the door of the attorney's office. Knocking, she was surprised when the door instantly opened. The man who opened the door wasn't what she expected. Mr. Montgomery was a short, pudgy man. He didn't wear a business suit, and he didn't seem stuffy at all. He was older and had a short goatee around his mouth. His hair was pulled back into a ponytail at the back of his neck, and he smiled when he saw her.

"You must be Amanda. You look just like your father, except for your eyes. You have your mother's eyes. Let's hope you didn't inherit your father's temper, though," he chuckled.

"You knew my father?"

"Oh, why yes, my dear. We grew up together, Josh and I. Have to say we got into a lot of trouble as kids, and your aunt Mabel was always there to wag her finger and tell on us. You see, there were the three of us; Joshua, Jeremiah, and I. We were called the three musketeers. Mabel wanted to be the fourth, but you know boys. We would never let her, so she always ran and told on us to get back at us for not including her; the little minx." He told the story fondly, and she instantly knew that this man held her family in the highest regard. She also knew he was her ticket to finding out the truth about her family.

"Do I have any more family that I don't know of?" She held her breath, as though she were a child again, asking if Santa Claus was real.

"I am sure you do, my dear. Unfortunately, your aunt was the last of your father's line. She couldn't have any children, and most of the family was killed in a fire in '90. I am sure there is still family on your mother's side, though. However, I must warn you that they are not the kind of people you want to know. Now, if you will come in, I will tell you about everything that now belongs to you."

"What?"

"Oh, my dear, you must know that your father's family had a legacy. You are the only Traverse left to take over the family business."

"What? I don't know what you're talking about."

"They never did tell you who you really are, did they? Oh, you poor child. I am afraid you are going to learn some things about yourself that are going to be hard for you. You must still be a virgin as well."

"I beg your pardon, sir, but I don't see how that's any of your damn business."

"No, my dear, I do not mean to be crude. I was just saying that you have never undergone the Change. It will happen, though. You recently turned twenty-four, and everything changes now."

"What change? What in the hell are you talking about?"

"They hid that from you, too? Oh my gosh. You don't know? Oh, Lord. Okay, first things first. You are now the owner of your family's estate."

"Family estate? So I have a house."

He smiled kindly at her. "Not just a house, my dear. It is what holds the legacy of your family name together. The estate has fifteen bedrooms with their own bathrooms and fireplaces, a kitchen, dining room, parlor, living area, office, library, Carolina room, staff quarters, wrap-around porch with two different sections screened in, pool, tennis courts and 300 acres. It was the pride and joy of your ancestor, Edgar. He was a distant grandfather of yours."

"Oh my gosh."

"Yes, ma'am. How about this? How about I get the keys and directions to the place? You go take a look at it, and then we can talk tomorrow about what you want to do. Stephan has been looking over things, and since your aunt's death, he has given everyone time off until you arrive and decide where to go from there."

Amanda wasn't sure she had the energy to deal with all of this tonight. "Unfortunately, it is very late. Is there somewhere that I can stay for a couple days and then I can go from there and take the day tomorrow to go look at the place?"

"That is perfect. Just give me a second, and I'll find a place for you to stay tonight."

Amanda sat quietly and listened to him talk on his phone. She didn't even hear his words as she thought of what she was going to do.

"I have gotten you a little cabin to rent down the road," he said, drawing her attention back to him. "It is in the woods a little but has electricity and such. On such short notice, I couldn't find anything else. It is only about ten minutes away. The key will be under the mat at the front door. Just go on in and make yourself at home."

"That is perfect. Thank you so much."

"You're welcome, my dear, and we will talk tomorrow. Say ten o'clock tomorrow morning? We will meet here and go to see the house together."

"Perfect. Thank you, Mr. Montgomery."

If you enjoyed this sample then look for **Romeo Alpha: A BBW Paranormal Shifter Romance - Book 1.**

Here is a preview of **another story** you may also enjoy:

KRISTIE LOOKED at the sky as she pulled up in
front of the casino. The air was chilly and the clouds
were dark and threatening snow, which was the last
thing Kristie felt like dealing with. She had been in her
car for over ten hours, driving home from college for
the holidays. Her back was sore and her legs needed to
be stretched out. She wanted a hot bath in a Jacuzzi tub.
She'd settle for a hot tub. But who was she kidding?
There was no hot tub to be found at her parents' house
and trying to have a hot bath without being interrupted
was almost impossible.

Kristie had approached the holidays with an ever-
growing sense of dread. It wasn't that she didn't want
to see her mother, but every time she came home, it was
like being suffocated. Her hometown had held more
appeal for her when she was younger, back when her
father was alive. Since he'd died and her mother had
gotten remarried last year, Kristie had delayed going
home at all. She had only met her step-father in passing
and hadn't met his nephew, who he tried to raise on his
own.

Kristie had saved up to stay at a hotel the entire
break. It had made the most sense to her. It would cause
the least amount of stress during her stay and give her
space when she needed it. But when she had mentioned
this to her mother, there was no way to mistake the
sadness in her mother's voice for anything else.
Knowing she was upsetting her mother by refusing to
stay at home with her new family, Kristie had cancelled

the reservation and agreed to stay at her mother's house instead.

She looked up at the casino where her mother had worked the last five years. Her mother worked in the back offices, far away from the lights from the slot machines and the sounds of people winning money. The casino was a little run down but brought in a steady stream of people who could afford the middle-level slots and risks it provided in a town that was mostly quiet.

The stale smell of cigarettes and alcohol hit Kristie in the face as she stepped inside. She looked around, seeing if anything had changed since the last time she had been here. Nothing jumped out of her. A few of the slots seemed to have been upgraded, but the carpet was still worn down and dirty and the place had an air of despair that made Kristie's skin crawl. She had never been to Las Vegas, but she imagined that the casinos there weren't as depressing.

Kristie made her way to the back and asked for her mother through the grate where an attendant was standing, looking at her cellphone. The woman went off to find her mother, and Kristie was soon ushered into the back offices. The casino décor quickly ended back here. Her mother's small office was near the back, shoved in a corner. The door was ajar, and Kristie peeked her head in.

Her mother was looking at the computer, squinting through her glasses to whatever was on the screen. When Kristie knocked on the door gently, her mother looked up and smiled. Kristie was startled to see she was going gray. The last time she had seen her mother, she had been a brunette. It was odd to see age creeping up on her. She came over to her and hugged her tightly.

"It's so nice to see you again."

"You, too, Mom."

Her mom urged her to sit down as she sat across from her at her desk. It made Kristie feel odd, as if she was interviewing to be her mother's daughter. Her mom didn't seem to notice, however, and smiled again. They made small talk for a while, mostly talking about Kristie's experiences at college. Kristie felt tired. She knew her mom meant well, but she really wanted to go home and nap. She was only here to get the address to her mom's new place.

"How are things with Lionel?" Kristie finally asked, feeling as if she didn't bring up her mom's new husband, she would never get out of the tiny office.

Her mom seemed to relax now that Kristie had brought him up, "He's great. Really, we're just wonderful. There are some issues, though…"

"Like what?"

"Well, it's actually one of the reasons that we wanted you to stay with us instead of a hotel. See, Lionel's nephew, Gray, is a bit of a handful. Lionel still feels responsible for him since he became his legal guardian when Gray was just a little boy."

Kristie wasn't following, "Okay…"

"He tends to run on the wrong side of the law, and we thought it'd be so great if you two could meet and maybe hang out."

The words hung in the air. Kristie felt a twinge of annoyance. She had thought her mother wanted her at the house because she had missed her, not because she wanted her to play nice with her new step-father's nephew. They weren't in grade school anymore. Trying to change someone set in their ways by sticking them with a goody-goody was a useless attempt.

Kristie took a deep breath and held it for a few seconds, letting the air out slowly. Her mother watched, a worried expression on her face.

"What do you want me to do with him?" Kristie finally asked.

Her mom, taking the fact that Kristie hadn't said no as a good sign, started to ramble. "Well, maybe just hang out with him. Show him what you do for fun. Maybe you two can go to the movies or something."

Kristie raised an eyebrow, "Go to the movies? What does this guy do for fun anyway that has you two so stressed out?"

Her mom avoided her stare and sighed, looking tired. "He runs with a bad crowd and doesn't like to listen. He's a good kid though. He's just lost."

"And you think I can fix him?"

"It wouldn't hurt to try, would it, Kristie? For me?"

Kristie sighed and nodded in agreement. How could she say no to her mother? She would always wish that her mother hadn't gotten remarried, but she didn't want her mom to be unhappy either. Her mom got up and walked over to her, hugging her tightly. Her mother's hugs had always reminded Kristie of being a little kid, outside playing till the sun set and running back inside for dinner. Back when her father was alive. Kristie shut her eyes tightly, willing the memories to leave her. She didn't want to think about her father right now.

Her mom finally pulled away and looked at her, smiling, "We'll have to really talk, you know, all about college and everything."

"Yeah, of course."

Her mom's eyes swept down her quickly, so fast that if Kristie wasn't used to it, she never would have picked up on it. She steeled herself.

"Maybe you and Gray can go to the gym. It'd get him out of the house and you could lose a few pounds at the same time," her mom said cheerfully.

Kristie mumbled in agreement and gave her mother one last hug before leaving the office. She should have known that there wasn't going to be any way in hell that her mother would have let an entire conversation go without making some sort of remark to her about her weight.

As she trudged through the casino, her mood lowered with every step. She regretted coming here for the holidays. Before her, they spread out in a bleak landscape. Dealing with her mother's 'helpful advice' in regards to her weight, and trying to show her loser relative by marriage around town. At the very least, she should have kept the hotel reservation.

Kristie dragged out the drive toward Lionel's house. Her mother had given her the address and it was close to the casino. A ten-minute drive didn't seem like enough time to prepare for whatever she was going to walk into. As she turned down the street where her mom's new house was, she found herself taking a deep breath. The first time, she just drove past the house. It was non-descript and had nothing of worth showing that made Kristie even notice it. Her mom had stopped gardening after her father died, and the front yard of this house was plain and dull.

Kristie pulled into the driveway. The garage door was open and a man was underneath a truck, working on it. She could only see his feet. Kristie got out of her car, grabbing her bags, and looked inside the garage. The man didn't look up when she shut the door of her car.

"Hello?" Kristie called out toward the man under the truck.

He didn't answer. Heavy metal was blasting out of a stereo nearby, but it was such an old stereo that the music sounded tinny. Kristie called out again, but the man still didn't answer. She knew that he heard her because he stopped working at one point and went still before resuming. She hoped this wasn't Lionel, because the guy was an asshole. *Probably his fantastic nephew.*

Kristie trudged toward the front door, leaving the other guy behind. What a fantastic trip this was going to be.

If you enjoyed this sample then look for **Devil's Advocate: A BBW MC New Adult Romance Series - Book 1 by Carla Coxwell**.

Other Books by Darla Dunbar

- The Romeo Alpha BBW Paranormal Shifter Romance Series (This series precedes the "Romeo Alpha Blood Lines Romance Series")

- The Alpha Feud BBW Paranormal Shifter Romance Series

- The Alpha Packed BBW Paranormal Shifter Romance Series

- The Daemon Paranormal Romance Chronicles

- The Mind Talker Paranormal Romance Series

- The Leather Satchel Paranormal Romance Series

Get the latest update on new releases from the author at:

https://darladunbar.com/newsletter/

About the Author - Darla Dunbar

Darla has been interested in paranormal romance since she was a teenager in high school. It was then that she discovered she could fulfill her fantasies through her writing.

Observing people and human behavior in the area of romance has always been one of her favorite pastimes. Combining that with an overactive imagination is a sure fire way of coming up with interesting themes.

Connect with Darla Dunbar

I really appreciate you reading my book! Here are my social media coordinates:

Friend me on Facebook:
https://www.facebook.com/darladunbar/

Follow me on Twitter: https://twitter.com/DarlDunbar

Check me out on Goodreads:
https://www.goodreads.com/author/show/8425857.Darl
a_Dunbar

Subscribe to my newsletter:
https://darladunbar.com/newsletter/

Visit my website: https://darladunbar.com/